Binding Vows

Gayle Roper

AnniesFiction.com

Books in the Inn at Magnolia Harbor series

Where Hope Blooms
Safe Harbor
Binding Vows
Tender Melody

. . . and more to come!

Library of Congress-in-Publication Data
Binding Vows / by Gayle Roper
p. cm.
I. Title
2019930120

AnniesFiction.com
(800) 282-6643
The Inn at Magnolia Harbor™
Series Creator: Shari Lohner
Editor: Lorie Jones
Cover Illustrator: Bonnie Leick

10 11 12 13 14 | Printed in China | 9 8 7 6 5 4 3 2 1

Merlyn

As Merlyn Marshall regarded the magnificent Magnolia Harbor Inn, she felt like Scarlett O'Hara about to enter Tara but without the corset, the petticoat, or the eighteen-inch waist.

She couldn't believe that she got to stay at this gorgeous place for five whole nights for free. All she had to do was smile and wear the dress in robin's-egg blue that she'd found for twenty-five dollars at the consignment store.

Not that she'd tell anyone, especially Paige Reppert, where she'd discovered the lovely dress or what she'd paid for it. Both would probably be grounds for being sent home.

Merlyn climbed out of her battered but loyal Honda Civic and leaned against the little black car, studying the inn. Big white columns supported impressive verandas that ran the length of both the first and second floors. Boxwoods and azaleas edged the porch, and long windows welcomed the warm June sunlight. Great oaks shaded the impeccably landscaped lawn.

Wonderful and magical things could happen in a place like this. No bitterness, no fear, no hurt was allowed here. Just anticipation. For the first time in weeks, Merlyn felt a spark of hope. She couldn't stop the smile that spread across her face.

She remembered the phone call she'd received last month that had brought her here.

"I want you to be my bridesmaid," Paige had said.

Merlyn had pulled her cell phone from her ear and stared at it. The beautiful princess was asking her, the late-blooming class dweeb, to be in her wedding? She imagined Paige with a long list of friends to ask to be her attendants, and Merlyn's name was at the bottom. How many people had turned Paige down before she was desperate enough to ask Merlyn? She hadn't even known Paige was engaged.

But then her own personal life had demanded all the attention she could give it, and her emotions were too fragile to take on someone else's concerns, good or bad.

"It's going to be a destination affair in a barn in South Carolina," Paige told her with no real excitement in her voice.

"It sounds lovely." To Merlyn, even the barn part sounded great, though she had a hard time picturing Princess Paige in her couture wedding gown sharing space with cows and horses. Still, anywhere away from Reynolds—both the town and the person—sounded wonderful. And she'd never been to South Carolina. However, traveling to another state and buying a bridesmaid's dress would be expensive, and Merlyn couldn't afford it.

Before she could come up with an excuse to say no, Paige said, "My parents are paying for the whole thing for everyone in the wedding party."

"Everything? For everyone?" Merlyn asked. Surely, she'd heard wrong.

"Rooms, food, entertainment—everything. All you have to do is get a dress, and you can pick any dress you want as long as it's robin's-egg blue."

Merlyn loved that color. It made her eyes look bluer than normal.

"And get a pair of nude shoes," Paige added.

Thank goodness Merlyn already had a pair. She'd bought them when she had a regular income.

"The place we'll be staying is on the water," Paige continued. "Bring your bathing suit."

So here Merlyn was in Magnolia Harbor, South Carolina, at this incredible inn, bathing suit stuffed into her suitcase. She'd expected to stay at a generic chain hotel on the water, which would have been fine. But this was something else entirely. For someone with only $359.74 in the bank and rent due next week, it was an unexpected thrill. Even three months ago when she'd still had a job, a fiancé, and money, it would have been wonderful.

She reached into her Civic, grabbed her purse, and climbed the inn steps, still unable to believe she would be staying here. She looked up and down the spacious veranda with its collection of chairs and chaise longues just waiting for her to collapse in. Her grin was so wide it made her cheeks ache.

Merlyn walked through the front door, and a bell chimed. She stopped in the impressive foyer and gazed around. A glittering chandelier hung over the gleaming marble floor, and a gracefully curving staircase made its way to the second floor. Oh, she could definitely get used to this.

As Merlyn turned to shut the door, she noticed a small brown-and-black dog with a white blaze on his chest had followed her inside. She bent and scratched his head. "I don't think you should be in here, little guy."

He gave a woof and trotted to the woman walking into the foyer.

The woman scooped up the dog and smiled at Merlyn. "I'm Grace Porter. Welcome to Magnolia Harbor Inn. I see you've met Winston."

"Winston, huh? As in Churchill?" Merlyn studied the dog. "That's a big legacy for a little guy to carry."

Grace scratched behind the dog's ears. "You live up to it, don't you, Winston?"

Winston wriggled, and Grace set him on the floor. He ran to

Merlyn, sat down, and held out his paw.

Merlyn laughed and shook his paw. "He's adorable."

"He's that and much more," Grace said, her voice warm with affection. "He thinks he owns the place, but he's so cute we don't mind. Come on, Winston. Let's get our guest checked in."

Minutes later, Merlyn followed Grace and Winston up the stairs and down a hallway.

Grace opened a door and stood aside. "Welcome to the Bluebell Suite."

When Merlyn entered the room, she let out a great sigh of pleasure.

Grace smiled. "I love the reactions people have when I show them their room."

"It's gorgeous." Merlyn couldn't decide which feature she liked most. The king-size bed with the tufted fabric headboard and crisp white bedding? The lovely blue walls that had likely earned the room its name? The chandelier hanging in the center of the room with its sparkling crystals that cast rainbows on the walls? The fireplace set with blue-and-white tiles? Or the claw-foot bathtub right in the bedroom? "I love the tub."

"It's all yours." Grace crossed the room and opened a door. "You share the bathroom with the Rosebud Suite."

At the word *share*, Merlyn felt a momentary twinge of concern. Which of Paige's mean girlfriends would she have to tiptoe around? Then she caught herself. High school was ten years in the past. Whoever was in the Rosebud Suite would have changed since then. After all, she had changed.

Merlyn was no longer the girl from the wrong side of the tracks. Not that the tiny town of Reynolds, North Carolina, had any railroad tracks to be from the wrong side of. Still, everyone back home knew about her growing up in a well-worn trailer park with a missing father and a mother who spent more time with friends than feeding her daughter.

But that was then. These days Merlyn had a handsome fiancé named Reynolds Coltrain, and she was a partner in a growing Web design company with a good salary, a fancy apartment, and a closet full of expensive clothes.

Merlyn blinked back tears as she corrected herself. She had been engaged to Reynolds, and she had been a partner in a growing Web design company with a good salary, a fancy apartment, and a closet full of expensive clothes. She still had the clothes, though she thought often about selling most of them. And she still had the apartment, at least until next week when she wouldn't be able to pay her rent.

At least she wasn't back in the trailer. Yet.

Deep breath. Don't go there. She'd survived when she was a kid, and she'd survive now.

With her chin high and shoulders back, Merlyn followed Grace downstairs to retrieve her suitcase and laptop from the car.

Grace smiled. "In an hour, my sister, Charlotte, and I will be serving afternoon tea with her delicious pecan sandies and petit fours on the veranda."

Merlyn had seen beautiful pictures of afternoon tea in women's magazines, and she'd always wanted to go to one. "Hat and gloves required?"

Grace laughed. "It's come as you are."

"That's good because I didn't pack them," Merlyn said, smiling. "How about scones and clotted cream?"

Grace nodded. "And lemon curd and homemade strawberry jam."

"The tea?"

"Earl Grey, English Afternoon, and vanilla lavender."

"And I have to choose?" Merlyn asked.

"You can have a cup of each."

"That sounds amazing. I'll go get settled now." Merlyn walked outside to her car.

Winston followed her, watching from the veranda as she removed her suitcase from the trunk and set it by the steps.

"Guard it for me," she told the dog. "I'll be right back."

Winston came down the steps and sat beside the suitcase, appearing alert and on duty.

"You, my boy, are the best."

He gave her a big doggy grin.

Merlyn climbed into the car and drove to the parking area. When she got out of the car, she gazed across the back lawn at Lake Haven. It was a stunning blue under the friendly dome of a sun-drenched sky, so perfect it took her breath away.

She still couldn't believe she was staying here. An afternoon tea was on the agenda, and who knew what other interesting experiences were in store for her? She hoped she would have some free time to sit on that inviting veranda and heal.

Thank You, God! Thank You, thank You, thank You! I need this so much.

A frenzy of sturdy barks and high yaps drew Merlyn's attention.

Winston had abandoned his guard duties and was racing across the lawn, his little legs a blur.

A black puli, his corded dreadlocks flopping around him and making him resemble a mop gone mad, followed—or maybe chased?—the smaller dog.

Winston caught sight of Merlyn and veered in her direction. The next thing she knew, he was behind her legs and half under the Civic. He lay panting, clearly expecting her to defend him from his pursuer.

As the puli rushed toward her, she thought about jumping into the car, but that would leave Winston exposed. Besides, she loved dogs.

She wouldn't have reached maturity reasonably sane if not for her fox terrier. How many nights as a kid had she cried herself to sleep, tummy growling, arms wrapped around her sweet Trixie?

Merlyn studied the puli as he drew to a stop in front of her. No signs of intent to harm. It seemed like the opposite. The dog's dreadlocks shimmied with a life of their own as he wagged his tail in delight at meeting her. His lolling pink tongue and white teeth were the only things visible in the black mop. "You're amazing," she told him.

He must have agreed because the wagging intensified.

She held out her hand, his friendly manner taking away any apprehension, and the puli edged closer. She patted his head and was surprised at how soft his coat was.

Winston peered out from behind her legs.

"You're scaring this little guy," Merlyn said to the puli.

The puli looked at Winston and dropped his front end so they were eye to eye. He gave an encouraging bark that Merlyn interpreted as an invitation to friendship.

Winston glanced up at her as if he wasn't sure.

"Locky!" a woman called, hurrying across the lawn. "Locky, where are you?"

Merlyn straightened. Sonja Reppert, Paige's mother, always had that effect on her. She was everything Merlyn's own mother wasn't—capable, caring, and involved with her children. And that was just the beginning of the list.

"Do you belong to her?" she whispered to the puli, indicating the woman with a tilt of her head.

"Locky! Come to Mommy!"

Merlyn blinked. *Mommy?* Plenty of people used baby talk with their dogs, but it was more than a little surprising to hear it from Mrs. Reppert. Merlyn always thought that if Paige was the princess, Sonja was the queen. Queen Sonja, regal and serene. Hearing her refer to herself as Mommy, and to her dog no less, was like seeing Queen Elizabeth skip as she inspected the troops.

The puli glanced over his shoulder as he heard Mrs. Reppert's voice, gave a happy bark, and ran to her.

Mrs. Reppert bent and scratched behind the dog's ears. "You bad boy," she said without heat. "Mommy was worried about you."

Elegant in her periwinkle-and-white linen outfit, Mrs. Reppert walked to Merlyn. The woman's hair was cut in a spiky do that was redder than Merlyn remembered, but other than the potential hair coloring, she appeared remarkably unchanged. The few times they'd interacted when Merlyn was growing up, Mrs. Reppert had always been kind to the kid from the trailer park, kinder than Paige and her friends had ever been.

Now charm oozed from her as she said, "Marilyn, how wonderful to see you. I'm so glad you were able to join us."

Marilyn. She got that a lot with such an unusual name. Merlyn made herself smile. "Hello, Mrs. Reppert. It's very nice to see you too. It's been quite a while. And it's Merlyn."

Mrs. Reppert blinked. "What did I say?"

"Marilyn."

"Well, yes. What should I have said?"

"Merlyn, two syllables." She knew she was being foolish. Churlish, even. What did it matter if Mrs. Reppert mispronounced her name? On the other hand, her name was just about the only thing she owned right now.

"Merlyn, two syllables," Mrs. Reppert repeated. "Like the magician at Camelot. I'll work on remembering."

Merlyn was impressed with Mrs. Reppert's gracious manner at the correction and embarrassed at her own pettiness. There was no way she could explain that Merlin the magician spelled his name with an *i* while the very nonmagic Merlyn spelled hers with a *y*.

Mrs. Reppert glanced at the Honda, and Merlyn wondered what she thought of the beat-up car. Merlyn felt like reaching out and patting the old thing like a cowboy might pat his horse. Three months ago, she'd been driving a black BMW with every upgrade known to man. Reynolds had leased it for her in the company's name. He'd reclaimed the car when he'd pulled off his hostile takeover. Sue Ann Chalmers drove it now.

Her Civic might be well past its sell-by date, but it was dependable and all hers. "My well-worn car."

Mrs. Reppert smiled. "And it got you here in one piece. What more can we ask of our vehicles?"

Merlyn nodded and gestured toward Locky, who was still trying to make friends with Winston. "I love watching his dreadlocks flap when he runs."

"Yes, his corded coat is unique to his breed."

Corded coat, not dreadlocks. She needed to remember that.

"James named him Locky after his coat."

James as in Mr. Reppert? Locky as in dreadlocks? Merlyn hid her surprise.

Mrs. Reppert glanced down at her dog. "You're our good boy, aren't you, baby?"

Locky squirmed with joy.

Mrs. Reppert transferred her warm smile to Merlyn. "Anyway, *Merlyn*, two syllables, I'm so glad you could be here for Paige. She's always treasured your friendship."

That wasn't the way Merlyn remembered it, but she managed to smile and say, "It's an honor to be in her wedding."

Mrs. Reppert nodded as if that was a given, but the light in her eye indicated she knew a line when she heard one.

Merlyn swallowed, searching for something to say that was actually the truth. She indicated the inn. "This is a beautiful place."

"Isn't it? They had a cancellation for a family reunion when the patriarch died suddenly, and we were able to step in."

"How sad for them," Merlyn replied. "But this place is perfect to host a wedding party, isn't it?"

"There's just enough rooms for you girls." Mrs. Reppert gestured toward the shoreline. "James, Locky, and I are staying at a cottage on the lake. We thought you girls would have more fun without us, so the inn's all yours."

"That was thoughtful." *Expensive but thoughtful.*

"There should be a schedule of events in your room," Mrs. Reppert said. "Dinner tonight is dressy casual."

Merlyn nodded. She remembered seeing a slip of paper on the bed. At least she had the right clothes for a dressy casual dinner after her years with Reynolds.

"This whole wedding has happened so fast, and Paige has been very emotional. We must hurry, hurry, hurry because she can't live without Drake." Mrs. Reppert frowned. "Tell me, who names her baby boy after a duck?"

Merlyn couldn't help but grin. She'd often wondered how Reynolds's mother could name him after a town.

Mrs. Reppert flapped her hand. "Forget I said that. Drake is a very nice man, and I should know. He lived with us his senior year in high school when he aged out of the foster care system. He and Quint were friends, and they played together on the football team. Then Quint went off to college, and Drake went into the Army."

Merlyn's memory of Drake Fremont was a bit fuzzy. He was one of Paige's older brother's friends, seen at a distance as they all grew up.

Tall, sandy-haired, quiet, at least compared to the exuberant Repperts, he had simply been there, a steady presence with a pleasant manner. He'd been the lineman who protected quarterback Quint the year the team went to the state finals. They didn't win, but the players were hailed as heroes anyway. She hadn't known that Drake had been in foster care or that he'd lived with the Repperts.

Now that she thought about it, she wasn't even sure what Drake did for a living these days. If she were to pick a husband for Paige, it would be a type-A guy with enough brass to stand up to the princess, not a "very nice man."

Merlyn stopped her train of thought. At the moment, she didn't have the strength to worry about someone else's potential issues. All she could focus on were her own responsibilities of wearing the dress, carrying the bouquet, and smiling.

Mrs. Reppert furrowed her brow. "It's Paige who concerns me."

Merlyn didn't know how to respond. In school, Paige had always operated on the assumption that everything would go her way—and she'd been overwhelmingly right. Merlyn could only imagine how her expectations were disintegrating under the pressure of a rushed wedding, leaving her usual attitude in the dust.

"By the way, I've been waiting and watching for you," Mrs. Reppert said.

Merlyn blinked. "Watching for me?"

"Yes. You're here at my suggestion."

Merlyn would have thought Mrs. Reppert barely remembered her. She imagined her saying, "Oh, Marilyn Marshall? The poor kid from the trailer park? I think she used to be in Paige's class, didn't she?"

Mrs. Reppert tangled a hand in Locky's coat. "Quite frankly I told Paige if she wanted this wedding, she was to ask you to be one of her bridesmaids."

So Merlyn hadn't been at the bottom of Paige's list but the top of her mother's. Which was worse?

Mrs. Reppert's gaze bored into Merlyn. "You're here because you're reliable, intelligent, low-maintenance, and high-class."

Merlyn stared at her. She would have taken a step back if the car hadn't blocked any movement. Had she heard right? She'd always thought that despite her kindness, Mrs. Reppert had always seen her as the poor kid who was well beneath her daughter. She was Trailer Girl whose own mother treated her with indifference.

Then came another distressing thought. If lowly Trailer Girl wasn't how Mrs. Reppert viewed her, where had that idea come from? Was that how she saw herself? Now there was something to contemplate on a sleepless night, of which she had many these days.

"You're here to help keep Paige . . ." Mrs. Reppert paused as if searching for the correct word, then cleared her throat. "Grounded. Yes, let's say grounded. It's a kind way to put it."

Merlyn winced. Grounded like a lightning rod so the building didn't burn? She was to draw the emotional strikes and thus protect Paige from combusting?

"She needs a friend who has no hidden agendas. Someone honorable and intelligent." Mrs. Reppert patted Merlyn on the arm. "You."

2

Merlyn

As Mrs. Reppert and Locky wandered off, Merlyn gave Winston a quick ear rub and reached into her car to grab the dress hanging on the hook in the back seat. With her laptop bag in one hand and her dress in the other, she walked back to the inn and her waiting suitcase.

So babysitting Paige was the cost of this elegant vacation. In her own way, Queen Sonja had paid her wonderful compliments. Low-maintenance and high-class. Reliable and intelligent. Merlyn didn't usually feel any of those things these days. She was more prone to feel stupid, gullible, and defeated.

She pulled up the handle of her suitcase and rested the laptop against it. She bumped her way up the front stairs, through the lobby, and to the second floor. When she entered her room, it took her breath away again. It was so pretty.

Merlyn noted the schedule of events on her bed. She glanced from the schedule to her watch. Afternoon tea would be coming up soon.

She took a quick shower in her shared bathroom without seeing whoever it was she was sharing with and slipped into the terry-cloth robe that waited for her in her closet.

As she walked into her room, she stopped when she saw a large rectangular box on her bed. It had appeared while she was in the bathroom. Someone had been in her room when she was at her most vulnerable. Merlyn shivered and pulled her robe's belt tighter, then hurried to check that the room's door was locked. It was.

17

Whoever had come in had had a master key. She couldn't decide whether that made her more uncomfortable or less. She walked to the bed and saw her name written on the front of the box. At least she suspected it was meant to be her name. *Marilyn.*

Mrs. Reppert had been here?

It must be something for the wedding. Merlyn slid the top from the box and was greeted with a sea of tissue paper. She pushed it gently aside and found a dress in robin's-egg blue.

Had she misunderstood about getting her own dress?

As she gently pulled the garment from the box, she felt her stomach drop.

Ruffles, ruffles, and more ruffles. It was as if the dressmaker had been challenged to add ruffles wherever possible and had risen to the occasion. There were ruffles everywhere. At the neck. At the hem. At the wrists. Even down the front from shoulder to waist in a *V*. And not pretty airy ruffles of a chiffon-like fabric either. Overwhelming ruffles. Ruffles that devoured the person inside them.

She glanced at the closet, where she'd hung her twenty-five-dollar dress. It was classy and classic, a dress that was as right for her as this new one was wrong.

Merlyn was petite, only five foot two. The profusion of ruffles on the dress would make her look like a four-year-old who was allowed to pick her own party dress in a store that specialized in over-the-top styles. All that was missing were the sparkly sequins and glitter.

Had the Repperts gotten this for her because they thought she couldn't afford a dress on her own? She made a face. That meant they knew the humiliating story of Reynolds and R&M Design. But of course they knew. What was she thinking? Everyone in the town of Reynolds had heard her story. It was one of the joys of living in a small town.

She had to find out if there were similar dresses waiting on the beds of the others in the wedding party. The afternoon tea took on a deeper significance than simply easing her hunger. It would allow her the chance to gather information. But what if no one but her was "blessed" with a dress?

Were the Repperts being kind, thinking she couldn't afford a decent dress? If so, how could she reject the gift without seeming petty and ungracious? But did they really think something this atrocious was a style she would like?

Merlyn took a deep breath. She reminded herself that a wedding was about the bride and her wishes, not about the bridesmaids. A woman should get exactly what she wanted on her wedding day.

How about the day a woman lost her fiancé, her job, and her income? Not to mention her self-respect? Nothing she got that day had been what she wanted.

And lay off the self-pity. It's not becoming.

She dropped the awful dress over her head. With any luck, it would be the wrong size.

Unfortunately, it fit perfectly. Merlyn gawked at herself in the full-length mirror on the inside of her closet door. She could hear clotheshorse Reynolds whooping with laughter and imagine Sue Ann smirking at his side. She shuddered at the thought of them watching her march down the aisle resembling an escapee from an eighties girl group.

A terrible thought struck her. What if Reynolds and Sue Ann were also in the wedding? She rubbed her hands up and down her suddenly chilled arms. Reynolds was Drake's good friend, and Sue Ann used to be one of Paige's best friends in school. She could remember the two of them with their heads together as they paraded through the halls giggling at misfits like her.

Merlyn couldn't believe that she hadn't thought of the possibility before. She chalked it up to being put on the spot when Paige had called her and everything else she'd had on her mind lately.

She glanced at her image again and sighed. So she had to wear an overabundance of ruffles. So Reynolds laughed and Sue Ann smirked. It was only for one day, and she didn't have to pay for the outfit.

Her breath caught. She didn't have to pay for it, did she? In a mild panic, Merlyn examined the box, tossing the tissue paper aside as she hunted for a bill. When she found none, her breathing slowly returned to normal. Embarrassment she could live with. Another debt she couldn't.

Sinking despondently onto the bed, she almost sat on a smaller box she'd missed before. It was square and deep. With trepidation, she opened it. A little birdcage hat sat on a crumpled ball of tissue to keep the veil from wrinkling.

She removed the hat and studied it. A silk flower decorated it, but she couldn't tell what kind of flower it was supposed to resemble. The hat was sort of adorable, but whether it would still be cute with the dress and all its ruffles was another thing. She walked to the mirror over the small chest in the room and put the hat on.

Merlyn slapped her hand over her mouth to stifle a laugh. With her curls frizzed out by the humidity, the small hat perched on her head looked like a blue basketball net. The veil wasn't full enough for her to pull over her abundance of hair.

Maybe if she arranged her unruly mop into a bun, the birdcage would fit. She pulled her hair back and held it at the nape of her neck with one hand while she put on the hat with the other. Even before she had it situated, her curls sprang free, forcing the hat to roost on the top of her head like a demented bird.

There wasn't enough hair spray in the world to fix this.

Paige had told her the bridesmaids would wear a ring of fresh flowers in their hair. She said it would be a halo of daisies and rosebuds with a ribbon woven through and hanging down the back. Merlyn could do without the ribbon, but the flowers had sounded nice, especially with the bouquets matching the wreaths.

After Merlyn put the robe back on, she hung the ruffled dress next to her twenty-five-dollar treasure. She returned the birdcage to its box and stashed it on the shelf in the closet. *Out of sight, out of mind.*

She redid her makeup with the ridiculously expensive stuff she'd charged to her credit card without any premonition of coming catastrophe. These days she could barely afford a tube of lipstick from the drugstore.

As Merlyn brushed her hair, she studied the thick, naturally curly mass. Containing it was an ongoing challenge. It was longer than she liked, hitting her shoulders instead of skimming her jawline. She'd last had it cut before Reynolds had made his stealth attack. She shook her head. Nothing could have surprised her more than finding the office door locked.

Don't go there. Sufficient unto the day.

She tucked her hair behind her ears in a futile effort to control the wayward curls. She shrugged. It was what it was. Gone was the pricey salon where she'd regularly had her hair cut to keep its stylish edge. Another secondary loss, along with her weekly massages, manicure and pedicure appointments, and sessions with her personal trainer.

Next, Merlyn dressed in indigo linen slacks and a rose-colored silk tunic with a dramatic asymmetrical hemline. She slid her feet into her navy sandals. Her hair might run riot, but her wardrobe was second to none, thanks to Reynolds, who had impeccable taste.

She checked her watch again. She didn't want to be early going downstairs, but she didn't want to be late to the party either. Pushing her shoulders back and raising her chin, she opened the door and stepped into the hall.

At the same time, the door to the room beside hers opened and a woman with brown eyes and short dark hair entered the hallway.

Relief coursed through Merlyn as she greeted Ashley Petersheim. She knew and liked Ashley. She had been friendly to everyone in school, even the class dweeb. Sharing a bathroom with her wouldn't be a problem.

"How wonderful to see you." Ashley gave Merlyn a warm hug. "Isn't this the most amazing place?"

Merlyn returned the hug. "I've never stayed at such a fancy inn before, and I plan to luxuriate. There's a bathtub in my room."

"Then I call the gorgeous one in our bathroom."

"It's yours as long as you promise not to use all the hot water," Merlyn teased.

Ashley held up her right hand like the good scout she was. "On my honor."

Merlyn grinned. "You seem happy. Life in Charlotte must agree with you."

Ashley's smile dimmed a bit, and a sadness quickly swept across her face. "Work's fine. I'm fine. It's all fine."

Merlyn frowned. It sounded like Ashley's life wasn't going so well either.

The door across the hall opened, and Sue Ann Chalmers walked out—all five feet eight inches of her. Her long blonde hair hung straight and shining down her back.

Merlyn froze. Even though she had considered the possibility that Sue Ann would be in the wedding party, it was still startling to see her. Then she realized that no one had told her. No, it was worse than that. Paige and Mrs. Reppert had deliberately withheld the information. Did they think Merlyn wouldn't come if she knew?

"Hey, Ashley," Sue Ann chirped. "Don't you look great?"

"Thanks," Ashley said. "You too."

As Sue Ann gave Ashley a big hug, she stared at Merlyn over Ashley's shoulder and gave her the very smirk Merlyn had been thinking about a few minutes ago. She also rested her left hand on Ashley's back so the put-your-eye-out diamond on her third finger was obvious. Sue Ann released Ashley and aimed a phony smile in Merlyn's direction. "Merlyn."

"Sue Ann." Merlyn's heart pounded, and her stomach cramped. Suddenly afternoon tea seemed inedible, no matter how lovely it had sounded when she'd been talking to Grace.

Sue Ann strode off down the hall and knocked on the other door on her side of the hall.

Hailey Madsen stepped out wearing a green silk sheath. It screamed designer—expensive designer—and her gold necklace must have also cost a fortune.

As much as Merlyn hated to admit it, Hailey was beautiful with her sleek highlighted bob and perfect figure. That brilliant shade of green might have been made for her. But who was she trying to impress? It was only the bridesmaids attending the afternoon tea.

Until this evening and dinner with the men in the wedding party. That undoubtedly meant Paige's older brothers, Quint and Colton, would join Drake. Merlyn hadn't seen the brothers in years since they'd both moved away from Reynolds for their jobs. There should also be one more man to complete the wedding party. Merlyn had the sinking feeling that it would be Reynolds.

Sue Ann leaned close to Hailey, her hand raised as if to cover her mouth, and whispered something. Hailey glanced in Merlyn's direction, then nodded at Sue Ann. All that was missing was the teenage giggling.

Ashley reached out and grabbed Merlyn's hand, offering her a sympathetic smile.

Merlyn shrugged, but her eyes felt teary from Ashley's kindness.

She held back a moment, blinking furiously, amazed and grateful when Ashley waited with her. Merlyn could certainly walk onto the veranda alone, but it would be so much easier with someone at her side.

Merlyn tapped a finger beneath her eyes. "Mascara?"

Ashley smiled. "It's fine."

They followed the others down the lovely curving staircase.

Merlyn should have known that the free stay in this gorgeous inn was too good to be true. There was always a price. Always. Sometimes it was ruffles. Sometimes it was being genial in the face of not-so-subtle snubs. Sometimes it was grounding a princess.

She determined to find the courage to pay the steep fare. It would be step one in reclaiming her life.

Grace

Grace Porter surveyed the back veranda as she and Winston waited for the young women who were part of the Reppert wedding party to arrive.

The refreshments table was a visual and culinary delight. Vases containing yellow, cream, and deep-pink roses provided pops of color. Elegant dishes held petit fours, pecan sandies, and scones. Next to the scones were cut-glass bowls of clotted cream, lemon curd, and homemade strawberry jam. Salted cashews, almonds, and tea sandwiches with their cucumber-and-cream cheese or chicken-salad fillings offered an alternative to the sweets. Skewers of assorted fruit rested on a colorful platter. Bowls of sugar cubes, small white pitchers of milk, and a plate of lemon slices waited to be dropped into the tea as desired.

But the pièce de résistance was the charmingly mismatched floral teapots and teacups ready to serve the most important part of the event—the tea.

It wasn't often the Magnolia Harbor Inn served afternoon tea. Usually they served wine, cheese, and hors d'oeuvres to their guests each evening, but since the bride and her attendants were the only ones in the house, afternoon tea it was. If Grace and her sister, Charlotte, could provide what their guests requested, they did so with enthusiasm.

The wedding would take place four days from now in the barn, a building often used for group functions—everything from corporate events to family reunions. Paige's reception would also be held there, but a caterer from a nearby town had been hired to do the honors.

The word *barn* was a misnomer if ever there was one. Grace doubted that an animal had ever slept in the place, and the only animal who had even walked inside was Winston. The building was more rustic chic than true rustic. Chandeliers hung from the ceiling, and swags of white material were gracefully draped over the rafters. If the weather was pleasant, they opened the barn doors, and guests could stroll across the lawn to Lake Haven, slip into the Adirondack chairs, and watch the sun set over the water.

Grace walked to the pile of pink floral cloth napkins and carefully adjusted a corner of one napkin that was slightly out of line. She straightened the already straight stack of china luncheon plates that had once been her great-grandmother's.

"You should put your hands behind your back until the guests come downstairs," a familiar voice said. "Everything is exactly the way it should be. Leave it alone."

Grace turned to Charlotte, who had just walked onto the veranda. "Things can always be better."

The inn's front door opened, and their aunt, Winnie Bennett, breezed in wearing her walking togs. Winnie and her husband, Gus, lived less than a mile down the road, and she liked to route her daily walk so she could pop by the inn.

Winston went running to greet her.

She bent and scratched his ears. "My Phoebe sends her greetings," she told him.

Winston sneezed.

Winnie laughed. "Cats aren't on your favorites list, are they?" She straightened and smiled at Grace and Charlotte. "I had to stop by and take a peek at your afternoon tea."

"Charlotte outdid herself with all the goodies," Grace said.

"And thanks to Grace, it looks like a tea party fit for the queen,"

Charlotte added.

Winnie regarded the refreshments table. "Oh, girls, it's lovely."

"There are some extra petits fours in the kitchen," Charlotte said. "More pecan sandies too. Help yourself."

"It's tempting," Winnie said. "But I'd better not."

Grace had to admire her aunt's discipline. Winnie had type 2 diabetes, and she controlled it with diet and exercise. She herself planned to indulge as soon as the tea was over.

Winnie walked around the veranda. "This is family china," she said, touching one of the teacups. "Aren't you afraid it'll get chipped or dropped?"

"I'm not worried," Grace replied. "Besides, what good is it stuck in some cabinet somewhere?"

Charlotte nodded. "We decided to use it because it's perfect for a tea party."

Winnie smiled at Grace and Charlotte, her eyes slightly teary. "You girls amaze me. Your mother would be so proud."

The three stood silently for a minute thinking about Hazel Wylde, Winnie's sister and Grace and Charlotte's mother, who had passed away six years ago.

"So proud," Winnie repeated with a hug for each.

Voices drifted down from upstairs.

"Here they come." Grace went to the doorway of the veranda, prepared to greet each guest.

Charlotte took her seat by the hot teas. She would pour Earl Grey, English Afternoon, vanilla lavender, or the last-minute addition at the request of the bride's mother, peach blackberry.

Winnie walked across the back lawn, waving goodbye over her shoulder.

The first one to arrive was Paige Reppert, the bride-to-be, with her maid of honor, Sue Ann Chalmers.

Grace offered her best hostess smile. "Welcome."

Paige smoothed the front of her pretty pink-and-yellow sundress. She wasn't so much brushing at imaginary wrinkles as she was wiping her palms in a nervous gesture. She blinked often as if she wore contact lenses that bothered her, and her smile was marred by little nervous tics around her mouth.

In her time at the inn, Grace had seen more than a few brides, and Paige was one of the jumpiest she'd ever encountered.

Paige was an elegant young woman, with her blue eyes and honey-colored hair, graceful movements, and high style. Too bad any sense of joy was absent. She needed someone to hug her and tell her to relax and enjoy herself. After all, this was her party.

"Please help yourselves to the food," Grace told them, motioning to the refreshments table. "Charlotte will pour your tea."

Sue Ann smiled as she regarded the setup, the green lawn beyond the veranda, and the sunlight sparkling on the lake. "How beautiful." She brought her hands to her heart, the huge diamond on her ring finger nearly blinding in the daylight.

Paige and Sue Ann filled their plates and accepted their cups of tea from Charlotte. Then the young women walked to the table for six that Charlotte indicated and took seats beside each other.

A moment later, Hailey Madsen entered and made a beeline for the food.

As Hailey filled her plate, Merlyn Marshall and Ashley Petersheim walked onto the veranda, followed by Sonja and James Reppert.

Grace hurried over to greet the bride's parents, and Charlotte followed.

"Good afternoon." Grace gave the couple her best innkeeper smile. "We're really enjoying Paige and her friends."

"And preparing the tea for them was a wonderful change from

our regular routine," Charlotte added.

Sonja took in the scene and smiled. "Thank you. It's all I'd hoped for and more."

"I'm so glad you're pleased," Grace said, then turned to James. "Are you going to join us for tea?"

He shook his head. "I'm meeting the men for a round of golf, but Sonja insisted I check things out first. I think I'll snitch a few snacks and be on my way."

Grace laughed. "Help yourself."

They all went over to the refreshments table.

James grabbed a petit four and a couple of pecan sandies. After sampling each, he closed his eyes in pleasure. "So good."

Sonja patted her husband's arm. "There'll be some food for you at The Tidewater. Go have fun with the boys."

"Your wish is my command." James kissed Sonja on the cheek, then strolled away, humming.

Sonja watched him leave with a fond smile. When he was gone, she clapped as if saying it was time to get to work. "Excuse me while I say hello to the girls." She headed to the table where Paige, Sue Ann, and Hailey were seated.

Sue Ann and Hailey smiled at Sonja while Paige regarded her petit four as if an important life lesson were inscribed in the icing.

Ashley had filled her plate while Grace and Charlotte were talking to Sonja and James. Then she took her tea from Charlotte, walked to the table where the young women sat, and claimed the fifth and final seat.

The last one to collect her tea was Merlyn, the one who thought Winston was named after Churchill. The young woman moved toward the table, then hesitated when she saw all the places were taken.

Grace frowned. There had been six chairs at that table when she'd done the setup. Six. One for the bride, each of her four attendants, and

Sonja. One had been moved while she and Charlotte were talking with Sonja and James. She scanned the veranda and spotted the missing chair resting against the building some distance down.

Grace studied the young women seated comfortably at the table. She felt a slow burn as she understood Merlyn's exclusion. That chair had been moved with malice. She rushed to retrieve the chair, planning to put it back where it belonged.

Sue Ann turned to Merlyn with a smug expression and pointed to a four top across the veranda. "You can sit at that table. There are plenty of chairs over there."

Hailey pressed her lips together to stifle a smile, and Paige, who had turned her attention to her teacup, seemed either unaware or uninvolved in her friends' petty behavior.

Ashley rose and collected her plate, cup, saucer, and napkin. "I'll sit with you, Merlyn." She started toward the table Sue Ann had indicated.

"I'll join you." Sonja followed Ashley and Merlyn across the veranda. Before sitting down, Sonja paused and stared at her daughter, who continued to study her teacup. Since she got no response from Paige, she then glared at Sue Ann, who appeared to be in deep conversation with Hailey.

Grace exchanged glances with Charlotte, and her sister rolled her eyes.

Grace swallowed her irritation at the heavy-handed snub and approached Merlyn's table. She was relieved to see Merlyn, Ashley, and Sonja talking easily. She wanted to say there had been the right number of chairs, but she knew she'd sound defensive and unprofessional, so she bit back her need to declare herself innocent.

Instead, she asked, "Are you all settled in your rooms? Is there anything I can do for you?" *Maybe lecture Sue Ann and Hailey about pettiness and doing unto others as they'd want done to them?*

Merlyn paused with her teacup halfway to her mouth and smiled.

"My room is wonderful. I feel privileged to be staying here." She indicated the sweep of lawn to the water's edge. "And the view is amazing."

While Ashley and Sonja said pretty much the same thing, Grace studied Merlyn. Her comments had seemed genuine, offered in the easy manner of someone at home in social situations. What was the story behind the snub given her?

And if there was so much tension between the women, why had these four been invited to make up the wedding party?

4

Paige

Paige blinked and glanced up from studying the design on her tea-cup. Judging by her mother's stern expression, there would be a lecture in her future. She sighed and took a bite of a petit four. It wasn't her fault Sue Ann and Hailey were up to their usual tricks.

Still, she made to rise even as her mother, Ashley, and Merlyn took seats together.

"Don't," Sue Ann hissed. "Let them be."

Paige nodded. It was easier to give up than fight to get everyone together. Besides, she should probably cut Sue Ann a little slack. Having Reynolds's ex-fiancée here for the wedding had to make her uncomfortable. It was understandable that she didn't want to sit with her.

Well, Sue Ann would have to deal with it. For some reason, Mom and Dad had been adamant about Merlyn being one of the bridesmaids. They'd told her that Merlyn had to be included if Paige wanted them to pull off a big wedding in less than two months.

Not that Paige minded Merlyn's presence. She liked Merlyn. When they were kids, she'd felt sorry for her, living in that trailer park with her awful mother. Paige had laughed when Sue Ann and Hailey christened Merlyn *Trailer Girl*, but she'd never called her that.

As an adult, Merlyn had surprised everyone by doing so well until something went wrong at work and with Reynolds. Paige wasn't sure of the details, only the outcome. Merlyn lost and Sue Ann won. That was all she needed to know. With the chaos in her own life, she didn't have the energy to worry about Merlyn and her problems.

Sue Ann glared at the other table, then at Paige. "I don't understand why Merlyn's here. Since when has she become such a good friend of yours?"

Hailey laughed. "Does she make you nervous?"

"Do you really think I'm worried about her?" Sue Ann asked, flashing her diamond ring.

Hailey smirked. "Of course not." She gazed across the lawn to the lake and sighed. "This place is gorgeous."

"It is," Sue Ann agreed as she slid a piece of pineapple from her skewer of fruit. "The Dogwood Suite has French doors to the veranda. A great view of the lake. A king-size bed so big and comfy I might not get up tomorrow morning. A fireplace. Not that I need to use it with this hot weather, but it adds such a cozy feeling."

"I've got a fireplace in my room too." Hailey grinned. "And a lake view and French doors to the veranda."

"My suite's wonderful," Paige chimed in, forcing herself to be part of the conversation. "Besides the fireplace and comfy bed, there's a little alcove where I can sit and look out at the water and think."

Except she didn't want to think. She was happiest with her mind in neutral.

Paige wasn't sure how her mother had stumbled onto this inn, but she wasn't surprised that her parents would pull out all the stops for her. They'd treated her like their little princess her entire life. Paige assumed it was because she'd almost died when she was four. She'd suffered from some sort of flu, and she'd been sent to the hospital when her temperature skyrocketed to a hundred and five. For days, her parents had prayed for their only daughter's survival.

Paige had survived and been loved unconditionally ever since. Not that she hadn't been so loved before the illness, but their fear of losing her had crystalized their affection. Whatever Paige wanted, Paige got. It was a wonder she wasn't some entitled shrew.

Even her brothers, Quint and Colton, treated her like she was fragile. While the brothers of Paige's friends mocked them and teased them and spied on their dates, her brothers did none of those things. Instead, they encouraged her, watched over her, and gave her advice, most of which she blatantly ignored.

In turn, Paige loved her family. When friends complained about their parents and siblings, especially during their teen years, she never had a bad word to say about hers. Why should she grouse? They made her life exactly the way she liked it.

"Don't you agree?" Sue Ann asked. She stared at Paige, waiting for an answer.

Paige cringed. She'd been drifting again. It was a yes or no question. She had a fifty-fifty chance of answering correctly.

Hailey was watching her with a hopeful intensity she reserved for only one thing: Quint.

"Do I think Quint will finally notice you this weekend?" Paige asked, then held her breath.

Hailey and Sue Ann both nodded.

Paige released her breath. She'd guessed right. "Of course he will. Why wouldn't he? You're beautiful. He'll be knocked off his feet."

Hailey seemed to relax and went back to her food.

Paige didn't understand why Hailey was still so enamored with Quint. She'd been crazy about him since junior high. When they were high school freshmen, he'd left for college, and Hailey had moaned and wailed about it for months. The funny thing was that he'd never shown her any attention. He was too busy with his own life to notice his little sister's friend.

After college, Quint had surprised his whole family by joining the Navy with the goal of becoming a SEAL. And he'd done it. They'd all been so proud and scared. Not that they were ever told what he did or where he went, but they knew he was constantly in grave danger.

But Quint had resigned and come home as of last week. He was safe, and Paige could relax after ten years of constant worry.

Paige thought it interesting that Hailey had never yearned after Colton, who was every bit as special as Quint. Her brothers were both tall and handsome, with square jaws and broad shoulders just like their father's. Colton was doing very well for himself in their family's business. But Hailey told Paige that his work sounded boring, especially compared to being a SEAL. Of course, she'd never seen Colton on one of his overseas missions to bring safe water to villages that had no access to such a thing.

Oh, well, the heart wanted what the heart wanted. Paige should know.

When she'd told her parents that she wanted to marry Drake immediately, they'd been surprised.

"I didn't even know you were dating him," Mom had said.

"I've known him forever," Paige answered. "He was like another big brother."

"But how did he go from big brother to fiancé?" her mom persisted.

"That's a good question." Paige did her best to seem thoughtful. "I'm not sure I can explain, but sometimes the bolt from the blue just strikes."

"Well, he's a very fine man," Dad said. "But he's nice."

Paige laughed. "And that's bad?"

He grinned. "I realize that as a complaint about a future son-in-law, it is pretty ridiculous."

But she knew what he meant. She'd been raised in a family of strong, opinionated alpha men, and like her mother, she wasn't afraid to stand up to them. She'd have to be careful with Drake or he'd be eaten alive.

"Are you sure?" Mom asked at least once a week. "It's not that I don't like Drake. What's not to like? He's kind and generous and hardworking. He's used his vacation time to go to Africa on well-drilling trips with Colton and Dad. And I know he's a success as a salesman at the car dealership because he bought himself that lovely bungalow over on Persimmon Street. But are you sure?"

Paige smiled and nodded and said, "Of course. How could I not be?"

Now she looked at her plate. It was almost empty. If only she could remember whether the food had tasted good.

5

Merlyn

For a moment, Merlyn had stood motionless. She was suddenly right back in high school with the mean girls ruling the lunchroom. Only today's reaction to the pettiness was disbelief, not the hurt and humiliation she'd felt in the past.

It hadn't taken long to realize there had been six chairs at the table so everyone could sit together. A chair that matched the ones at the table was resting against the house farther down the veranda.

Merlyn glanced from Sue Ann to Paige to Hailey. Sue Ann and Hailey seemed much too pleased with themselves while Paige appeared lost in her own thoughts, evidently unaware of the face-off between her bridesmaids. Poor Ashley's face turned red, though Merlyn knew she hadn't done anything.

When Sue Ann said, "You can sit at that table," Merlyn made herself smile warmly despite the emotional chill in the air. She would not give the woman the satisfaction of seeing her true feelings, even the contempt she felt for such a juvenile trick. Eating alone at the table across the veranda would be awkward, but she vowed that Sue Ann would never see her discomfort.

"Thanks for the suggestion," Merlyn said with all the grace she could muster. "I think I will. The view from there will be spectacular."

Sue Ann blinked and stared. Obviously, it wasn't the reaction she was expecting.

And was that disappointment that flashed across Hailey's face?

Merlyn hoped so.

Then Ashley and Mrs. Reppert stood and sat with her in a not-very-subtle rap on the mean girls' knuckles.

They'd barely settled in their seats when Mrs. Reppert said, "I'm so sorry."

There was no need to pretend Merlyn didn't know what the woman was talking about. She shrugged.

"It's not just their rudeness I'm apologizing for," Mrs. Reppert continued. "I need to apologize for my own actions."

Merlyn was at a loss for words at how kind Mrs. Reppert was being to her.

"I should not have put you in this situation without warning you," Mrs. Reppert went on. "Without giving you a choice."

Merlyn had to agree, but she remained silent.

"I was afraid that if you knew Sue Ann and Reynolds would be here, you might refuse to come," Mrs. Reppert said. "I thought Sue Ann could keep her spitefulness under control."

"Spitefulness?" Merlyn thought a better word was *gloating*.

"And jealousy," Mrs. Reppert added.

"Jealousy?" Merlyn repeated. "What does she have to be jealous of? She's got the guy, the car, the ring, and the company."

"But wait." Ashley held up her index finger. "Does she really? If Reynolds cut you off, he could do it to her too, and she knows it. Sue Ann may lack many things, but intelligence isn't one of them."

"So she takes out her insecurities on me?" Merlyn asked.

Ashley nodded. "Because she's riddled with self-doubt."

"The way she struts around?" Merlyn scoffed. "I find that hard to believe. And it's nothing new. She's always been that way."

Mrs. Reppert took a sip of her tea, then held out her teacup and studied it. "The peach blackberry is very good. Have you tried yours yet?"

Merlyn got the memo. It was time to change the subject. "I got the Earl Grey. It's always good."

"I chose the vanilla lavender." Ashley inhaled the steam rising from her cup. "Just the smell makes me happy."

Merlyn remembered the flash of sadness that had swept across Ashley's face earlier and wondered about her claim to be happy. If there was any free time in the schedule, maybe they could have a pity party. *And wouldn't that be fun?*

What was genuinely fun was sitting with Ashley and Mrs. Reppert. It was much nicer than the six of them sitting together would have been. There was no tension, no worry about verbal jabs either subtle or overt. Instead, the three of them relaxed together, telling stories and laughing. They earned a few glares from the other table.

When Mrs. Reppert told a story about Locky running through the undergrowth in the woods and emerging covered with mud and burrs, Merlyn made a face. "How many hours did it take to clean him up?"

"It took forever, believe me." Mrs. Reppert smiled. "Fortunately, Locky loved all the attention."

"You have to meet Locky," Merlyn told Ashley. "He's adorable with all his dreadlocks. Oops, with his corded coat." She grinned. "Did I say it right, Mrs. Reppert?"

"You did, but either is fine. And please call me Sonja. You too, Ashley." A sparkle appeared in Mrs. Reppert's eyes. "That's Sonja, two syllables."

Merlyn had to laugh as Sonja explained the inside joke to Ashley. "All these years, I thought she was just saying 'Marilyn' too fast."

They all laughed.

"I mean it. Please call me Sonja."

Merlyn and Ashley glanced at each other. How did you begin calling a contemporary's mother by her first name?

But Merlyn understood the request was a compliment, so she said, "We'll try."

Sonja nodded, apparently pleased.

Even pleasant things had to end sometime, and eventually Ashley placed her napkin beside her plate and stood. "This was great. I loved both the tea and the company."

Sonja smiled as she rose. "I've enjoyed eating with you girls too. Thanks for including me."

Merlyn took her last sip of tea. "I should be saying thanks to both of you for saving me."

"Thanks all around," Ashley said as she pushed her chair under the table.

"Remember to be at the dock by eight o'clock for the ride across the lake to the restaurant for dinner," Sonja said. "We're eating late because of our tea and the guys' golf."

A ride in an open motorboat. Merlyn didn't want to think about what the wind would do to her already uncontrollable hair.

"Excuse me while I go speak with the others." Sonja gave them a wink, then walked away.

Merlyn rested a hand on Ashley's arm to stop her from leaving. Now was the time to ask about the ruffled dress. She hadn't felt free to say anything while Sonja was present because she didn't want to appear unappreciative if Paige had decided everyone should wear matching dresses. "Did you find a dress for the wedding on your bed?"

"What do you mean?" Ashley asked.

"Someone left a dress and a birdcage hat on my bed," Merlyn replied.

Ashley shook her head. "The only thing on my bed was the schedule." She frowned. "We were supposed to get our own dresses, weren't we? Did I misunderstand? Color was the big thing, not similar styles."

Merlyn exhaled in relief. "You didn't misunderstand. I bought my own dress too. And I love it."

She felt like turning cartwheels of joy. She didn't have to wear that awful dress. Or did she? If Sonja or Paige had gotten it as a kind gesture, she'd have to wear it.

Merlyn studied Sonja with her spiky hair and beautiful dress in shimmering shades of green and blue. She didn't look like someone who bought endless ruffles. And Paige was inhabiting her own nervous world where doing for others wasn't high on her list. On the other hand, she seemed all about the wedding. If she thought the dress would make the wedding better . . .

"Do you think someone left it in your room by mistake?" Ashley asked. "Maybe it belongs to one of the other bridesmaids and got put in the wrong room."

Merlyn shook her head. "The box had my name on it. *Marilyn.*"

"Ah, Marilyn, three syllables." Ashley glanced across the veranda. "That narrows down the field."

Merlyn had to laugh. "Well, it was after I talked to Sonja, so we know it wasn't her, don't we? When you see it, you'll understand why I don't want to wear it."

"Come on," Ashley said. "It can't be that bad."

"Believe me, it can. Would you like to take a peek?"

"Sure. Now I'm intrigued."

Merlyn ushered Ashley upstairs to her room. She made a show of opening her closet and removing the ruffled dress.

Ashley gasped at the dress on its hanger. "Wow. It is as bad as you said. Maybe even worse."

"When I put it on, it practically eats me," Merlyn said, holding the dress up in front of herself. "I'm much too short for all the ruffles."

Ashley shook her head. "That's not Paige's taste at all."

"That's the problem. I don't think it's anyone's taste." Merlyn put the dress back in the closet. "What makes me shudder is the idea that someone thought I'd love it and be thrilled to wear it."

With a laugh, Ashley returned to her room.

After Merlyn closed the door, she wondered what to do next. With dinner so late, bedtime would be later than she was used to, so she decided to take a nap. She grabbed her cell and set the alarm for ninety minutes. She might not sleep that long, but she mustn't sleep longer. Then she slid beneath the covers and fell asleep.

Half an hour later, Merlyn awoke but felt too lazy to get out of bed. She propped herself up against the pillows and admired her suite. She couldn't imagine having a room like this to come home to every day. Her apartment was really nice, and the furnishings were modern—all matte surfaces, sharp corners, and severe lines. Basically, she'd bought what Reynolds told her was smart and classy. She loved her apartment because it was a giant step up from the trailer, not because she felt comfortable and at home there.

Reynolds taught her how important image was. "Always buy quality. It's worth every penny. People can tell." He helped her buy quality even as the charges mounted on her credit cards. "You are your own best advertisement" was one of his favorite lines.

He was certainly his own best advertisement. "Reynolds Coltrain?" people would say. "Handsome. Charming. Funny. Delightful. Clever." And she had to agree. He was all those things.

But recent events had redirected her thinking, and she belatedly realized no one said, "Reynolds Coltrain? A man of character. A good man. An intelligent man."

Merlyn gave a snort of disgust, not with Reynolds but with herself. She was the one who had been foolish enough to be hoodwinked by image. She was the one who hadn't valued substance. That little girl from the barely livable trailer had been too excited that one of the town's young men of position had fancied her. Even though he was a dirty rotten scoundrel, she was the fool. It was debatable which of them was more pathetic.

Finally, Merlyn got out of bed and redid her face and hair. She grabbed her e-reader and went out onto the back second-floor veranda. What a beautiful vista.

The *snick-snick* of toenails heralded Winston, who came up to say hello.

"How are you doing, sweet boy?" Merlyn asked.

He wagged his tail and gave her a doggy smile.

"Aren't you hot in that fur coat?"

The dog flopped at her feet and panted.

Merlyn laughed.

As she gazed at the view, she noticed Paige walk out onto the lawn below and trudge toward the lake. Where were the excitement and joy a bride should feel a few days before her big day?

Sonja stepped onto the veranda and took the chair beside Merlyn. She greeted Winston and patted her knees. "Want to sit on my lap?"

Winston didn't hesitate. He jumped up and cuddled against her.

When he settled, Sonja rubbed his ears. "Neither of us can tell Locky about this, you understand?"

Merlyn chuckled, then sobered as she watched Paige drop into an Adirondack chair at the lake's edge. "Is Paige all right?" The question popped out without forethought, and Merlyn wanted to bite her tongue. She anxiously waited for Sonja's reaction, hoping she hadn't offended her.

Sonja sighed. "To be truthful, I don't know. About two months ago, she went on vacation with some girlfriends from work. She had such a good time that she stayed a few extra days. When she returned, she was suddenly in love with Drake. She had to get married immediately.

I asked her why she wanted to rush into it, and she told me that she desperately loved him."

Merlyn frowned. There was something desperate about Paige, but she wasn't sure it had anything to do with love. Or Drake.

A motorboat approached, heading for the dock at the foot of the lawn.

"Our transportation for dinner has arrived." Sonja set Winston down and stood. She turned, and Merlyn saw her face was tense with worry. "Please be there for her."

Merlyn

The motorboat from The Tidewater was sleek and fast.

Merlyn observed the driver as she and Ashley took seats in the bow of the boat. He was ruggedly attractive with a strong jawline and deep-brown eyes the color of his somewhat tousled hair. As soon as the boat pulled away from the dock and he sat on the driver's seat, head above the windshield, she understood why his hair was tousled.

Sonja sat in the most sheltered seat beside the driver and behind the windshield. Age and paying the bills did have their privileges.

The others crowded in the rear of the vehicle. As the boat flew over the water, Sue Ann's long blonde hair whipped wildly, slapping her and Paige in the face. Hailey was the smart one with a scarf tied over her do.

Merlyn let her curls fly. She threw her arms wide, tilted her head to the sky, and closed her eyes, enjoying the speed and the wind in her face. The joy of the moment temporarily reduced Sue Ann and Reynolds to mere bumps in the road.

"It's like flying!" she called to Ashley over the sound of the motor and the wind.

Ashley smiled back, that hint of unhappiness showing despite her smile.

I really need to find out what that's about, Merlyn thought.

The ride was over much too soon. The boat slowed down and drew up next to The Tidewater's dock in a smooth, easy motion.

Mr. Reppert and the wedding party men were waiting and waved a greeting. Drake and Reynolds tied the boat securely fore and aft.

Merlyn stood and moved with Ashley to the back of the boat to wait her turn to disembark.

Drake smiled and put out his hand to help Paige step onto the dock. Still holding hands, they walked up the path to The Tidewater.

Reynolds reached out to take Sue Ann's hand, then helped her onto the dock. He wrapped his arms around her and lifted her off the ground. They kissed enthusiastically.

Merlyn turned away and gazed out over the lake. She was surprised to find her chief emotion wasn't hurt or distress but annoyance. Sue Ann didn't have a subtle bone in her body, and Reynolds acted as if he were playing a role in an insipid rom-com.

Be careful, Merlyn warned herself. *Contempt is just as ugly as bitterness.*

When she turned back, a strong hand reached to help her. She took it, climbed onto the seat, and stepped onto the dock. She smiled her thanks and realized it was the driver who had assisted her. She glanced from him to the boat and back again. "How did you get on the dock ahead of me?"

"Agility. I simply stood on my seat and got out."

Merlyn smiled, amused. Since he was tall, the step that was so easy for him would have been difficult for her.

He grinned at her. "I thought about rushing to the back and pushing you aside so I could get out the traditional way before you. You know, so I could play the gentleman coming to your assistance."

Merlyn laughed. "Wouldn't the pushing have negated the assisting?"

"That's why I'm glad I saw a better way." He held up his hands. "In my own defense, though, it would have been a gentle push. I wouldn't want you going overboard."

"How kind and considerate," she teased.

"Don't make the mistake of thinking I'm too noble. I just didn't want to have to dive into the lake to rescue you. Wet clothes at dinner would be uncomfortable."

Merlyn glanced down into the water. "It's maybe three feet deep."

"Well, you are short."

They grinned at each other, and Merlyn realized he was still holding her hand. She tugged ever so slightly, trying to reclaim it discreetly.

He gave her hand a little squeeze and released her.

Now what? It had been so long since she'd had a silly, spontaneous, and slightly flirty conversation with a man that she'd forgotten how to extricate herself gracefully. Her gaze fell on the boat, and she latched on to the handy topic. "So will you be taking us home later?"

"I will."

"Good," Merlyn said, then flushed. It sounded like the good was for him, not the ride. It was, but she shouldn't let him know that, should she? "Well, it's a nice boat."

His eyes twinkled as he said, "Thanks. I enjoy it."

"It's yours?" She'd assumed it belonged to the restaurant.

"It is, and I enjoyed watching you enjoy the ride. I suspect you're a speed junkie."

Merlyn ran her fingers through her hair to try and tame it a bit. "I don't like speed in the car, but I love it in a boat. It's like flying but without the possibility of plummeting to earth from outrageous heights."

"Do you water-ski? It's the same sensation but stronger."

She felt more than a little skeptical. "I don't know if I'd like that. With the boat, I don't need any talent or training. I can simply sit back and enjoy."

"You're not telling me you're afraid to water-ski, are you?"

Merlyn recognized the challenge in his voice. "Maybe."

"Does tomorrow afternoon sound okay for your first lesson?" he asked.

She swallowed. Her stomach churned at the thought of trying to stand on two pieces of composite while flying over the water, all while he watched. She blurted out the first excuse she could think of. "I'm not sure what's on the schedule for tomorrow afternoon."

He shrugged. "Who cares?"

"Paige." And Sonja whose deep pockets came with obligations for Merlyn. How could she be a lightning rod protecting Paige if she was off drowning with this charming guy?

"Don't worry," he said. "I'll take care of her."

"Oh, Quint." The sultry voice was femme fatale smooth and steeped in coyness.

Both he and Merlyn turned to the voice. Now she knew who the driver was: Paige's older brother Quint. No wonder he thought he could ignore the schedule.

Hailey smiled warmly at him, ignoring Merlyn as if she were invisible. Big surprise. How were some women always so neat and put together? Hailey's hair was perfect, courtesy of the colorful scarf trailing gracefully from her hand, and her green silk dress wasn't even creased at the hips from sitting.

Merlyn sighed. Was there a charm school somewhere that she'd never been invited to attend? She was probably a disaster. Her slacks were linen. Enough said when it came to wrinkles. Her tunic didn't seem too bad, but she was sure her curls writhed about her head like Medusa's snakes.

"Walk with me, Quint?" Hailey purred. "These heels may be pretty, but sometimes it's nice to have someone to lean on." She batted her eyelashes.

Merlyn bit back the rumbling bubble of disbelief rising in her throat. Right here, today, on the dock of The Tidewater, the fight for women's equality had just been set back a hundred years.

Quint's quick glance and smile told Merlyn that he'd heard her snarky growl before she swallowed it.

As Hailey glided across the dock in her stilettos, Merlyn had to admire her. The woman was forced to walk on tiptoe so the skinny heels didn't fall through the narrow openings between the boards that made up the dock, and she somehow still managed to look as if she were floating.

Quint watched Hailey approach with a polite resigned expression that made Merlyn smile. She told herself she was a terrible person because it tickled her that he wasn't nearly as delighted to see Hailey as Hailey was to see him.

With a nod in his direction, Merlyn turned to walk up the path to The Tidewater, leaving him to his fate.

He reached out and touched her arm. "Tomorrow afternoon at one thirty. Your dock."

"I don't know," Merlyn said.

Quint laughed. "Don't worry. I won't let you drown."

"Promises, promises," Merlyn said. "Though that might be preferable to making a total fool of myself."

Hailey, who had been following their conversation with a frown, inserted herself neatly between the two. "I happen to know what's on the menu tonight," she told Quint as she took his arm. "You're going to love it."

Quint glanced at Hailey. "Excellent. I'm hungry." Then he looked over her head at Merlyn and winked.

Merlyn

Dean Bradley, the tall, slim owner of The Tidewater, warmly greeted them at the door and showed them to their seats.

Merlyn stopped when she saw the two tables set for six. What if she was at the table with Sue Ann and Reynolds? Her heart thumped uncomfortably at the thought. She might be able to handle one of them without having an emotional breakdown, but the two of them together with their lovey-dovey PDA would be too much.

There were name tags on the tables, and after checking them, Merlyn breathed a sigh of relief. The first table was the bride and groom, the parents, and the maid of honor and her fiancé. The other table was Merlyn, Ashley, Hailey, Quint, Colton, and a cute guy named PJ. She had no idea what PJ stood for. Peter John? Paul Jeffrey? Preston Joshua? Peyton James? Priam Jehoshaphat? Given his height and hers, she was willing to bet they'd be paired up for the walk down the aisle.

Quint ended up sitting between Hailey and Merlyn. Hailey seemed ready to purr like a cat who'd gotten the ideal spot before the fire. The table was small enough that conversation flowed easily with everyone included.

A couple of times Hailey tried to engage Quint in a more private conversation, but he gave her short answers. Merlyn could see that he tried to return to the whole group as quickly as he could without being impolite.

At one point, Merlyn noticed a look pass between Quint and Colton, just a slight widening of the eyes, and from then on, Colton would ask Hailey a question whenever she tried to cut Quint from the herd.

The dinner was excellent, prepared by a genuinely talented chef. First came freshly made vegetable spring rolls followed by a cup of beautifully made gazpacho. The mixed greens salad was topped with walnuts and pears and dressed with a champagne vinaigrette. The sorbet to cleanse the palette was a tart lemon, and the veal piccata with capers rested on a bed of angel-hair pasta. Dessert was peach cobbler in individual ramekins, made with locally sourced peaches.

Merlyn glanced at the other table when the veal piccata was served. She could imagine Reynolds pushing all the capers to the side and trying to keep his meat out of the delicious sauce. He was a finicky eater. At least there was nothing being served that would affect any of his allergies.

Beside her, Quint tucked into his food with gusto and asked the waitress to give his compliments to the chef on every dish.

After dinner, the group adjourned outside to enjoy the full moon shining on the lake.

Merlyn wandered down toward the dock with Ashley. She couldn't help but smile at Paige and Drake as they walked hand in hand. For once, Paige seemed to be engaged in what was going on as the pair talked with their heads together. Reynolds and Sue Ann trailed them.

"Does seeing Reynolds with Sue Ann bother you?" Ashley turned her back to them and began walking slowly in the opposite direction. "If it was my ex with another woman, it would certainly bother me."

Merlyn didn't respond as she matched steps with Ashley. How she appreciated a sympathetic ear. When Merlyn had told her mother what occurred, her mom had commented, "That's what happens when you try to be more than what you are. You got what you deserve."

Merlyn wrapped her arms about her stomach, still feeling the sting of those words. While she had endured years of being forgotten and overlooked by her mother, the meanness was new, born of jealousy at her success.

Her former success.

"When Reynolds first broke up with me, all I could do was cry," Merlyn admitted. "What had happened? How had it happened? Why had it happened? How could the man who asked me to marry him turn on me like he had? And what had I done to deserve it?"

"Have you gotten answers to your questions?" Ashley asked.

"I'm working on it."

"My advice? Don't waste your energy blaming yourself or trying to figure things out. Reynolds is just a user. He always has been."

"I realize that now, but how did I not know it before?"

"He's handsome and charming," Ashley replied. "Unfortunately, those two things hide a multitude of flaws."

Merlyn had to admit Reynolds's appearance and charm were the traits that had attracted her. She'd always thought he was incredible, one of those golden people way above her in their small town's hierarchy. In high school, she admired him as an older guy who knew his way around. But that way never included her, nor did she expect it to.

Then she worked her way through college in six years by clerking at night at convenience stores, waitressing, and doing whatever part-time jobs allowed her the flexibility to go to classes. Reynolds sailed through college in four years on his parents' money, spending his nights and weekends partying.

Four years ago, they'd bumped into each other at a seminar for small businesses. Merlyn was getting ready to transition from designing websites for friends for free to establishing her own business. She was at the seminar seeking ways to draw the attention of potential clients.

When Reynolds called after the seminar and asked her out to

dinner to talk strategy, she was amazed. As they compared notes about their dreams and goals, she started to view their meeting at the seminar as providential. He had the contacts she needed, and she had the skills he needed. R&M Design was established, and slowly their business partnership became more.

Merlyn froze as a terrible thought struck. Reynolds had used her and discarded her when he felt she had no more to give him. Had he planned it that way the whole time? Had he used her from day one? And how foolish did that make her that she'd never sensed it?

She shook her head. "I guess I only saw what I wanted to."

"A very human failing," Ashley said. "And Reynolds is skilled at projecting an image. You know what your problem is? You're not duplicitous, so you don't suspect it in others. You are what you are."

Merlyn gave a puff of laughter. "That's pretty much true. Still, I hate the thought that I was merely a handy stepping-stone to be kicked aside on his way to financial success. And a prettier fiancée."

"I don't know about prettier," Ashley said. "But Sue Ann's family does have money and position."

"I definitely can't compete there." Merlyn snorted. "And her engagement ring is much bigger than the one he gave me."

"I hope you kept yours."

"No, he asked for it back."

"Of course he did. How like him to make such a tacky move. He undoubtedly used it to underwrite Sue Ann's ring. You should be furious—I'm furious for you—and I don't mean just about the diamond."

Merlyn had to smile at Ashley's anger on her behalf. "At first, I was more shocked than anything. It was like the family's placid collie suddenly turned and took a chunk out of me. Total surprise, disbelief even. Betrayal."

"Yeah, but a dog's bite is quick," Ashley pointed out. "The kind of betrayal you suffered goes on and on, especially when you realize it was being planned long before you knew anything about it." She let out a long sigh. "That's what really hurts."

There was a wealth of personal experience in Ashley's words, which saddened Merlyn. She stared out over the lake, watching the moon's trail on the water. "There's one question I keep asking myself."

"What is it?"

"Was I so pathetic and grateful that someone as socially acceptable as Reynolds seemed to care for me that I didn't notice his disdain? It must have been there all along, but I never saw it." Merlyn shook her head. "The poor kid from the trailer park was too glad about finally being one of the cool kids to realize something was amiss."

Ashley patted her arm in comfort. "Some cool kids aren't worth our time and attention."

"Too true." Merlyn glanced back at Reynolds and was surprised to see that he and Sue Ann were no longer walking with Paige and Drake. Instead, they were mere yards behind her and Ashley. She couldn't even see Paige and Drake.

"This is a nosy question, and you can tell me it's none of my concern," Ashley said. "But how did he manage to get the business?"

"I've asked myself that question over and over. Basically, I was the creative half of the company, developing the sites and working with the clients," Merlyn began. It had hurt when none of her clients called to verify whatever it was that Reynolds told them about her. "Reynolds took care of the business side. At first I kept up with the contracts and finances, but when I got really busy, he told me he'd handle those details, which put me right where he wanted me."

Ashley nodded.

"He used to say to me, 'Don't concern yourself with the mundane. Let your creative talent flourish. I've got the rest.' I took what he told me as wisdom and trusted him. I never imagined he would turn on me. Never. Naive, stupid me."

Ashley swatted at a mosquito. "No, not naive or stupid. He was your business partner and then your fiancé. You should have been able to trust him."

Sue Ann's laughter, too loud and shrill, sounded behind them.

Merlyn swallowed the sour taste that rose in her mouth and tried to relax her suddenly tense shoulders.

Ashley rolled her eyes. "She wants you to hear how happy she is and be jealous of her. He wants you to know what you've lost." She gave a little snort. "They deserve each other, and you deserve much better."

Merlyn managed a small smile. "Thanks, but can you tell me why they care what I think? She's got Reynolds, and he's got the business. I've got nothing."

"Nothing but class."

"Class? Me?" *Trailer Girl? Really?*

"Absolutely."

Merlyn couldn't believe she'd received two compliments in one day. Sonja had said she was intelligent. Ashley said she had class. It didn't fix anything, but it did make her feel somewhat better.

"Can't you go after him in court?" Ashley asked. "It was your creative work that brought R&M business, not his math skills." She ducked and swatted at the air. "Mosquitoes are bad enough, but I hate bees."

Merlyn leaned away from the bee. "Don't we all? But I do like honey. We can't have one without the other."

Ashley ducked again. "I thought they didn't fly around at night."

"Obviously some do, or this guy didn't get the memo."

The bee dive-bombed Ashley one last time, then buzzed off to find another target.

From behind them they heard a shriek. "Bees!" Sue Ann sounded as if an entire swarm had descended upon her.

Merlyn spun around and saw Sue Ann swatting wildly. She felt her heart begin to race. "Sue Ann, stop!"

"She's going to get stung," Ashley said. She didn't sound too concerned.

"It's not her I'm worried about," Merlyn responded. "Reynolds is allergic to beestings. He gets hives and an erratic heartbeat, and his throat closes."

Reynolds slapped at his neck. Even with the distance between them, Merlyn noticed his eyes go wide.

He'd been stung.

8

Merlyn

Reynolds grabbed at his throat, which Merlyn knew was already beginning to close, making breathing more than a little difficult. Soon it would be impossible.

One of the first things Reynolds had done when they'd started working together was teach her how to use his EpiPen in case something happened to trigger one of his several allergies.

She'd had to use it once. They were in an upscale restaurant having dinner, and the waiter brought rolls with sesame seeds on them.

"I'm allergic to sesame seeds and oil," Reynolds told the man. "Do you have rolls without the seeds?"

"We do," the man said. "I'll get them for you."

In a few minutes, the waiter returned with a basket of rolls without sesame seeds.

Reynolds had buttered one of the rolls and taken a bite. Only seconds after swallowing, he'd grabbed his throat, which was already sprouting visible welts. Welts on the outside meant swelling on the inside.

Merlyn had taken his EpiPen from his pocket and stabbed it into his thigh right there in the fancy restaurant. In her haste, she'd knocked over her chair and sent a glass to the floor, where it had shattered. But his breathing eased almost immediately, and he hadn't collapsed into the shards of glass. Any semblance of a pleasant night out was shattered when the EMTs burst inside with a gurney, shoving tables out of the way so they could reach Reynolds.

It turned out the waiter had taken the rolls with the seeds into the kitchen, brushed off the seeds, and brought the same rolls back to the table, all bearing the sesame oil left behind when the seeds were brushed off.

Now as Sue Ann still batted at the bee, Merlyn saw Reynolds try to retrieve his EpiPen from his pocket. He collapsed before he could do it.

"What in the world?" Ashley sounded stunned.

"Anaphylactic shock." Merlyn edged toward him. "Get the pen, Sue Ann."

"Reynolds!" Sue Ann screamed. "What's wrong? Get up!" She glanced around, her eyes wild. "Someone help him! Call 911!"

"Get the pen," Merlyn mumbled under her breath as she took another step toward him. Surely, Sue Ann had had the pen lesson too.

But all she did was kneel beside him and cry, "Reynolds, don't die! Don't die!"

It was a nice sentiment but no help whatsoever.

Quint raced across the lawn with his phone in his hand. Paige and Drake were right behind him.

But Merlyn was closer, and she knew what to do. With a sigh, she sprinted to Reynolds and dropped to her knees.

He stared at her, fear in his eyes. "Help!" he wheezed.

Merlyn reached into his pocket and removed the EpiPen. "The least you could do is teach your new fiancée how to use the pen."

"What are you doing? Leave him alone!" Sue Ann reached across Reynolds and tried to push Merlyn away. "Get your hands off him! Someone get her out of here! Help him!"

Merlyn dodged Sue Ann and held up the pen. "Didn't he teach you how to use this?"

Sue Ann stopped screaming and gawked at the pen.

Merlyn removed it from its case and flipped off the cap. She grasped the pen in her fist and brought it down with force, stabbing it into his thigh. She began counting. "One, two, three—"

"You're hurting him!" Sue Ann shrieked, swinging at her. "Get away from him!"

Merlyn ducked again and kept counting. Sure, Reynolds had flinched when the needle struck, but was Sue Ann really foolish enough to think she'd harm him? And in front of an audience?

Ashley knelt beside Sue Ann and put an arm around her. "It'll be okay. She knows what she's doing."

Tears streamed down Sue Ann's face. "No, she's hurting him! Make her stop!"

Quint dropped down beside Merlyn. "I called 911. Help is on the way. Are you all right?"

After the emotional battering of the past few weeks, Merlyn yearned to drop her head onto his strong shoulder and feel safe and cared for. Instead, she nodded and kept counting. "Nine, ten." She held the pen in place a bit longer in case she'd counted too fast, then pulled it free and slid it back into its case.

Quint smiled at her. "Well done."

Her return smile was shaky.

Reynolds pulled in a breath. Over the next few minutes, his breathing continued to ease. By the time he was wheeled into the ambulance, he seemed much better. Merlyn noted that neither he nor Sue Ann even glanced at her. Nor had they thanked her for her help.

"I'm going with him," Sue Ann announced as she followed Reynolds to the back of the ambulance.

The driver shook his head and shut the door on her. "I'm sorry, but you're not allowed. Our insurance prohibits anyone but the patient and the EMTs from riding in the ambulance."

Sue Ann appeared lost. "But I'm his fiancée."

It struck Merlyn with the suddenness of a clap of thunder that the woman might actually love Reynolds. She'd assumed their romance was more for effect and personal gain, since both tended to be so narcissistic, but maybe it was real, at least on Sue Ann's part. Merlyn wasn't sure she'd ever trust Reynolds's motives again, and Sue Ann was still a thorn in her side, but maybe . . .

"I'm sorry," the ambulance driver repeated. "I couldn't let you ride even if you were his wife. No passengers. None. Only patients."

"But my car." Sue Ann motioned across the lake toward the inn. "How am I supposed to get to it?"

"We'll take you to the hospital," Quint assured her. "Let me get my car."

Hailey appeared at Sue Ann's side. "I'll come with you."

Quint scanned the crowd that had gathered around the ambulance. When he found Colton, the eye-widening thing happened again.

"We'll all come," Colton said. "Hailey, PJ, Paige, and Drake can come with me." He put his hand on Hailey's back and began urging her up the path.

"But . . ." Hailey's voice trailed off, and she pouted at Quint.

He ignored her as he addressed his parents. "Are you coming?"

"We'll drive ourselves," James said. "We'll let Locky out, then join you."

"Okay, see you there," Quint said. "Ashley, will you help Sue Ann?"

Ashley put an arm around Sue Ann's waist and led her toward the parking lot.

Merlyn witnessed Quint's tidy organizing of the troops with amazement.

Quint held out a hand to her. "And you're with me too."

Merlyn managed a small smile as she slid her hand into his. She was so weary. Spent.

"It'll all level out soon. You had an adrenaline rush, and now it's wearing off," Quint remarked, as if reading her mind. He guided her toward the car.

She walked quickly beside him. "When did you and Colton work out the eye thing?"

"What eye thing?" he asked.

"Innocence, thy name is Quint."

He laughed. "Is it that obvious? We've always thought we were secretive and clever."

"I'm sure you are," Merlyn said. "I happened to catch that look at dinner and observe the ramifications. I assume that if Colton does it, you come to his rescue too?"

Quint stopped for a moment and studied her. "You're very observant."

She warmed at the compliment. "If only that were true."

"You're talking about the R&M Design fiasco?" he asked.

Merlyn closed her eyes in pain. It wasn't physical pain, but acute embarrassment could hurt just as much.

Quint gave her a sympathetic expression. "I'm sorry, but it's a small town. Everything from Mrs. Westlake's hangnail to the latest business scandal is hashed over and over."

"I know."

"But you still saved Reynolds's life."

She shrugged. "Someone else would have if I hadn't."

"But you did." He squeezed her hand. "You did."

9

Ashley

Ashley Petersheim thought the evening would never end. She smiled. She conversed. She mingled. She thought she'd die.

But she was pretty sure she'd successfully played the part of a young businesswoman who lived in the city, where she enjoyed an exciting and fulfilling life. No one suspected the lonely, heartbroken woman who wanted to come home but couldn't because she was afraid that she might see him.

Ashley was glad Merlyn was here. She was ashamed that it wasn't because she liked Merlyn—she did—but because her recent and very public humiliation sucked all the oxygen from the room. So much attention and spite were aimed Merlyn's way that no one seemed to notice Ashley's subdued manner.

Poor Merlyn. Sue Ann's barbs and victorious attitude were bad enough. But now that Quint was smitten with Merlyn, she was suddenly in Hailey's crosshairs too. It was obvious that Hailey's sharp tongue and petty attitude were flaying Merlyn's already bruised spirit.

Keep them busy, Merlyn.

Not that Ashley wanted Merlyn to be hurt. She never wanted anyone to be hurt. From the first day of school when Paige had established herself as the kindergarten queen and Sue Ann and Hailey as her consorts, Ashley had decided to be nice to any of the girls—and boys—the trio deemed less than. She was also smart enough to know that she didn't want to be targeted, so she was nice to Paige and her friends too.

To the nicest girl in our class. That was a frequent message scrawled in Ashley's senior yearbook.

Nice.

As she finally dragged herself up the stairs at the inn well after midnight, she sneered at herself.

Nice.

What good was getting along with everyone when you were too nice to fight for what you wanted? Weak and pitiful were more accurate descriptions of her personality.

Ashley had to admit that dinner hadn't been too bad. The food had been delicious, and the conversation lively and amusing. She'd had a seat that put her back to the other table and the happy couple, and she'd managed to enjoy herself in an if-you-can't-see-the-problem-it-doesn't-exist kind of way.

After dinner, she and Merlyn walked along the waterfront in the opposite direction of Paige and Drake. Merlyn probably thought the choice of direction was to get away from Reynolds and Sue Ann and that Ashley was the epitome of considerate. If she only knew the truth.

It had been awkward sitting with everyone at the hospital as they waited for Reynolds to be released. He sat across the small waiting room from her, and he drew her eyes as light drew moths. Crossing or uncrossing his legs. Leaning forward to talk to another member of the group, his arms resting on his knees, head slightly cocked in that attentive way he had. He could make you feel your words were about to unlock the secrets of the universe and you were the most important person in the world—until he didn't.

As soon as Ashley entered her room and shut the door behind her, she wilted. She went to the closet and ran a hand down the blue dress she'd paid way too much for. She loved it. She looked great in it. There was nothing like appearing your best as your life was flushed away and your heart stomped on.

And wasn't she a drama queen? Except she wasn't. She was truly shattered.

She washed her face in the fancy bathroom and thankfully escaped to her room without having to talk to Merlyn again. She wasn't sure she could fake it another minute.

Ashley climbed into her big four-poster bed and sank into the fat pillows. She stared at the bouquet of pretty flowers—*alstroemeria?*—sitting on the mantel. They were so pretty. The wallpaper with the delicate red floral pattern was pretty. The windows with the frothy white drapes and red fabric valances were pretty. The fireplace with its lovely carved mantel was pretty.

Nice.

Pretty.

Bland words. How about some with real meanings?

Alone.

Rejected.

Tears trickled into her hair. She covered her mouth to muffle the ugly sounds she was making.

"I really enjoy being with you," he'd said to her only a couple of months ago, his wonderful soft-brown eyes smiling at her.

The words had given her such hope. Ashley hadn't told him she knew she was in love with him. She felt too uncertain of the depths of his feelings to say those words. *I enjoy you* wasn't exactly the firmest foundation on which to build a lasting relationship. But she knew on her part it was love. Would it have made a difference if she'd spoken her heart?

Spoken it before he said the words to one of her best friends?

She rolled over and sobbed into her pillow.

There was a knock on her door.

Startled, Ashley sat up and wiped her damp face. Who was at the door at this hour?

When another knock came, she realized it was the bathroom door. Merlyn.

"Yes?" Ashley called. Did she sound like a teary mess?

"Are you okay?" Merlyn asked.

"I'm fine. Just fine." Another of those bland, useless words.

"Oh," Merlyn said, doubt seeping into her tone. "You're sure?"

"I'm sure," Ashley said. "Good night."

There was a short pause. "Good night. Sleep well."

Ashley fell back on the pillows. "I'm fine," she whispered.

Nice.

Pretty.

Fine.

Nothing words for what had become a nothing life.

10

Grace

Wednesday morning at nine o'clock Grace sat at the desk, checking reservations for next week.

One couple was returning for their annual stay. They'd honeymooned at the inn five years ago and returned every year to celebrate their anniversary. Their days were spent relaxing and reading by the lake and strolling the cobblestone streets of Magnolia Harbor. They were both delightful, and Grace looked forward to catching up with them.

"Miss Grace, how wonderful to see you," a cheerful voice called.

Grace glanced up as Rochelle Earnhart burst into the room. She knew Rochelle from church and choir. Rochelle was also the county's most popular wedding planner. Grace was glad that she was coordinating Paige and Drake's wedding because she was pleasant and clever and always did a fantastic job. She created schedules for the event, timed the program down to the minute, and provided lists of everything expected from all participants.

Grace hugged her. "The ladies in the wedding party are finishing breakfast on the veranda."

"I know," Rochelle said. "I already said hello to them. What a beautiful group of young women."

"That they are," Grace said. "How are the plans for the big day coming?" She couldn't imagine pulling off a wedding in as little time as Rochelle had been given, but the wedding planner seemed to be taking everything in stride.

Rochelle beamed. "Everything's great. I stopped at the bakery before I drove out here. They're creating a wonderful cake with real flowers that match the bridal party's bouquets and hair wreaths."

"Sounds lovely," Grace remarked as she motioned to a chair. "Have a seat."

Rochelle sat down. "And the flowers are on order and will be delivered on time as long as no natural emergency interferes. They always give that caveat."

"I'm sure they have to."

"The bride was determined to have hydrangeas with her daisies and rosebuds." Rochelle made a face. "In South Carolina in June. Can you imagine?"

Grace hoped her face reflected the appropriate amount of surprise.

"The heat would have them drooping before the ceremony began." Rochelle frowned as if picturing the wilted blooms, but her smile quickly reappeared. "I wondered if I might take another walk through the barn if you don't mind."

"Of course," Grace answered. "You know you're welcome anytime."

"Great. Thank you."

Charlotte and Winnie walked in.

"How are you, Miss Winnie?" Rochelle rose and gestured to her chair. "Here. Have a seat. And, Charlotte, how wonderful to see you."

Grace got a kick out of Rochelle referring to her and Winnie as "miss" but not using the title for Charlotte. Undoubtedly that was because Charlotte and Rochelle were about the same age, but Grace and Winnie were old enough to be given the polite Southern manner of address. *There's a sobering thought.*

Winnie dropped into the vacated chair. "You'll never believe it."

From Winnie's tone, Grace knew something was wrong. She jumped up. "What happened?"

Charlotte waved dismissively. "Don't worry. We're not talking about a life-and-death situation. It's just that I've heard the most unexpected rumor."

"What rumor?" Grace asked.

"The caterer for the wedding is going out of business."

Merlyn

Wednesday morning when Merlyn walked onto the veranda for breakfast, she watched Sue Ann stiffen.

With her expression hard and her nose in the air, Sue Ann turned and marched back into the inn.

Merlyn was surprised to find herself more than a bit miffed at Sue Ann's behavior. Not that she'd expected she and Sue Ann would ever be friends, but after last night she had hoped for civility at least. When someone saves the life of the person you love, shouldn't you be grateful? Shouldn't you at the very least say thank you and behave politely toward that person?

Apparently not, at least in Sue Ann's world. In fact, the woman's dislike appeared to have escalated. Somehow it seemed to be Merlyn's fault that Sue Ann didn't know how to use the pen, and saving Reynolds's life was an insulting invasion of the couple's privacy.

Merlyn wandered to the table set for five and took a seat next to Ashley. "How are you this morning?" When she'd spoken to Ashley through the bathroom door last night, Ashley had stopped crying. But stifling tears didn't fix anything. Merlyn knew that all too well.

"I'm fine." Ashley gave her a huge smile. "Isn't it a beautiful day?"

So Ashley wanted to pretend that everything was going well. Merlyn gazed out over the lawn to the lake. "Absolutely gorgeous."

"Great for golfing," Ashley added.

Merlyn laughed. "If you say so. I'm not a golfer." Trailer park kids rarely were.

Paige strolled onto the veranda with Hailey and the previously retreating Sue Ann. They walked to the table and sat down, Paige at the head, Hailey across from Merlyn, and Sue Ann across from Ashley.

Grace served them glasses of orange juice, plates of stuffed French toast, and small bowls of honeydew wedges loaded with berries. The rainbow of colors brought Merlyn as much pleasure as the tastes.

Paige took a sip of her juice. She raised the glass and inspected it. "There's something in here besides orange juice. It's good."

"It's tangerine," Grace said as she reappeared with a carafe of coffee. She filled their cups, then walked away.

When Grace was gone, Ashley smiled at Sue Ann. "Wasn't it wonderful that Merlyn knew what to do last night?"

Merlyn wished she could kick Ashley under the table. Talking about last night was guaranteed to give them all heartburn.

Sue Ann fiddled with her fork, ignoring Ashley's question.

"What if she hadn't been there?" Ashley persisted. "Poor Reynolds might have died."

Merlyn's mortification was turning into amusement at Ashley's convenient overlooking of all the others present, though she was careful not to let her feelings show.

"How's he doing this morning?" Ashley asked Sue Ann innocently. "Are the hives gone? Is his breathing normal?"

"I spoke with him this morning, and he's fine," Sue Ann finally said, annoyance in her tone. "Thanks for asking."

"Oh, don't thank me." Ashley waved away the need for appreciation. "Thank Merlyn. If she hadn't been there—my goodness. I shudder to think what might have happened." She shook her head.

Sue Ann shot Ashley a lethal stare. The master manipulator had been manipulated, and she obviously didn't like it one bit.

Despite the awkwardness, Merlyn could have hugged Ashley. No one ever defended the trailer park kid.

Sue Ann took a deep breath and grimaced. "Thanks, Merlyn." She spoke to the air between Merlyn and Ashley, but at least she'd said it, even if she wasn't genuine.

Merlyn smiled brightly. "You're welcome," she said cheerfully. "I was glad to be able to help. I wouldn't want anything to happen to Reynolds." She managed to say the last sentence as if she meant it. She was a better actress than she'd thought.

Sue Ann chomped down on her French toast with enough force to crack a molar.

At long last, the uncomfortable breakfast ended and the other four women went to their rooms to get ready for golf. When they came back outside, they all wore sunglasses and sunscreen and carried their golf bags.

"So sorry you can't play," Hailey told Merlyn insincerely as they left. "We'll miss you."

Merlyn smiled and waved as they drove down the road. Sad to say, she wouldn't miss them at all. Well, maybe she'd miss Ashley and Paige, but it was still nice to be alone. She walked out to the dock and stood at the edge, soaking up the peace and quiet.

When she'd read that golf was on the schedule for this morning, she'd decided she wasn't even going to try. It would be the height of idiocy to expose her inadequacy to the capable and critical women here. Truth be told, she had a country club phobia. Even the thought of the public one the women would be playing at made her anxious.

Merlyn had dined at the local country club a few times with Reynolds as her escort. But she'd never had the time or inclination to learn to hit that tiny dimpled white ball. Besides, she hadn't wanted to use her hard-earned money for a membership when that same cash could grow her business. She sighed. Maybe joining the club would have been a better use of the money after all.

She thought about that idea for as long as it took her to blink. *Nah.*

Her negative feelings about the exclusivity of country clubs had been formed when she was in fifth grade. Paige had invited all the girls in the class to her big birthday party at Wessex Country Club, the town's private club with acres of greens, tennis courts, and a swimming pool. They were going to use the club's spa and get manicures, pedicures, and facials.

Thinking back on it now, Merlyn wondered why on earth ten-year-olds needed facials. But at the time, she'd been so excited to be included. She'd only heard of manicures and pedicures and had resolved to stop biting her nails so she'd have something to work with. And a facial. Movie stars got facials. Maybe hers would give her rosy cheeks that made her as cute as Paige. Well, not as cute. Nothing could do that. But maybe she'd be cuter than she usually was. She got goose bumps just thinking about it.

Merlyn had spent a considerable amount of time wondering what she should wear for this event. Princess Paige and her friends always wore the right clothes, and she tried to eavesdrop on their conversations so she could pick up a hint. She knew her usual always-too-short jeans and cheap T-shirts would be unacceptable.

Merlyn managed to talk her mom into driving to the strip mall one town over for a quick visit to the thrift shop there. The Wednesday before the party, Merlyn and her mom scoured the store and found the cutest outfit Merlyn had ever seen. It even fit well.

She held her breath at the checkout counter as they waited to see if Mom's credit card could take the cost. When the receipt printed out, Merlyn went limp with relief.

The day of the party she studied herself in the mirror in the bathroom. She had to climb on the toilet to see below her chest. When she grew up, she would get one of those long mirrors so she could see herself all at once. Merlyn smiled at her reflection, pleased at what she saw. She would look as nice as anyone for a change.

As Mom drove up the long driveway at the country club, Merlyn stared at smiling men in colorful clothes putting on the practice green. She'd never seen men in such clothes, but the colors made her happy.

Her mom snorted. "What kind of a twit wears lime-green pants with a pink shirt? And brown-and-white shoes?"

Merlyn didn't want the green pants, but the pink shirt with a collar and a little animal printed on it wouldn't be bad.

They also passed an outdoor pool with thick greenery hiding the fence surrounding it. It was full of kids splashing and women lounging in the sun. None of the ladies appeared to be swimming despite the swimsuits they wore. Maybe only kids were allowed in the water.

This privileged world was as foreign to Merlyn as Bora-Bora. She tried to ignore the butterflies in her stomach as they pulled up in front of the clubhouse with its white columns and deep-red shutters. She might never get to Bora-Bora, but she was here at the country club with all the popular kids, even if it was only for a couple of hours.

She climbed out of the car, a birthday gift she'd found at the thrift shop and a card in her sweating hands.

"Have a great time, toots," Mom called and drove off.

Merlyn waved and watched her drive away, telling herself she wasn't nervous about facing the unknown. She'd have a good time and pick a pretty nail polish for her manicure and pedicure.

"Toots?"

Merlyn's hands clenched around the present. She knew that sneering voice. She turned to see Sue Ann walking toward her.

A few feet away Hailey was holding open the clubhouse door for two of their classmates. All three were laughing.

Merlyn couldn't wait to laugh and enjoy herself, even if it meant spending Saturday with Sue Ann.

As soon as the door closed on the two girls, Hailey turned toward Merlyn, and her smile disappeared. She hurried to stand beside Sue Ann, and together they formed a blockade, barring Merlyn's way.

"Our job is to welcome everyone and tell them where to go inside," Sue Ann said.

Merlyn nodded. It was smart of Paige and her mom to think of that. If she just walked in, she wouldn't know where to go in a place this big.

"We're supposed to keep out nonmembers." Hailey's smirk clearly said Merlyn was in that group.

Sue Ann waved to the clubhouse and the pool and the golf course. "You have to belong to get in."

"You do not belong," Hailey stated.

Merlyn thought she might be sick.

Sue Ann reached out and took the gift and the card from her shaking hands. "We'll give these to Paige for you. I'm so sorry your mother left. Now you'll have to walk home."

Merlyn had already known she'd be walking home. Her mom was on her way to visit with friends. She'd have forgotten all about Merlyn by the time she should be coming to pick her up. But Merlyn hadn't thought she'd be walking home this soon.

"I-I have an invitation," Merlyn stammered, hating the quiver in her voice.

"That was a mistake," Hailey said promptly. "No one who lives in a trailer is allowed to be here."

Was that true? Was her invitation a mistake? Merlyn didn't know.

She did know you had to apply for membership at the country club, and if you were socially accepted, you had to pay lots of money. Was the rule Hailey talked about because trailer dwellers couldn't pass the social part or couldn't afford the membership fees?

Did it matter? Out was out, and there was no way to get in, not even if you had an invitation.

"Bye-bye," Sue Ann said as she tapped her foot impatiently.

Merlyn pressed her lips together. No way would she let them see her distress and aching disappointment. She should have known the country club wasn't for her. She'd been foolish to dream for even a minute that she'd fit in here.

If she did belong, she'd never, ever make someone who didn't belong feel the way Sue Ann and Hailey made her feel.

Merlyn forced herself to stand tall, though she wanted to crumple in a heap and sob. She turned and started down the driveway, blinking back tears.

The men in the colorful clothes watched her go. Now their smiles didn't seem pleasant but mocking. *Trailer Girl*, she imagined them thinking.

She should never have let herself dream.

"Oh, by the way," Hailey called after her, "that outfit used to be mine."

12

Merlyn

Enough with the maudlin memories, Merlyn chided herself. She was not going to sit around feeling melancholy when she was blessedly alone to enjoy this lovely morning. It would be hot and muggy by midafternoon, but right now it was perfect, not too humid with the temperature about eighty.

Winston trotted up, his nails clicking on the dock. He sat beside Merlyn and gazed out over the lake as if he was enjoying it as much as she was.

"I want you to be extra sweet to Ashley, okay?" Merlyn told him. "Cuddle in her lap or something. Make her feel loved. She's very sad."

Winston cocked his head as if asking for more information.

"I don't know what the problem is, though I suspect it's a man. Why else do women cry?"

Winston sneezed, and Merlyn took that as agreement.

"And Paige," she continued. "I don't know if she's crying too—she's on the third floor so I can't hear her—but something's not right there either."

Winston sighed and collapsed on the dock, resting his chin on his paws.

Merlyn grinned at him. "I know. It's more than I can handle too."

More clicking nails announced Locky's arrival. He dashed to the edge of the dock and jumped, hitting the water with a splash.

"Locky! No!" Sonja ran onto the dock, leash in hand, her face a picture of distress. "Oh, Locky, what have you done?"

Locky glanced up at her, his doggy grin in place. He swam to the lake's edge, climbed out, and shook himself. Water flew everywhere.

Sonja sighed. "With that thick coat, he'll be wet for ages, so I'll have to use the hair dryer on him. It'll take forever, and I have a meeting with the wedding planner in an hour."

"But Paige is golfing," Merlyn said. She assumed the bride would attend the meeting with the wedding planner.

Sonja didn't respond to the remark. Instead, she pressed her lips together as she watched Locky walk toward her. "Don't you dare," she warned the dripping dog as he tried to lean against her leg.

Locky started toward Merlyn, and she held up her hand. "No leaning here either."

The dog glanced from Merlyn to Sonja, realizing he was currently persona non grata. He seemed to be fine with that as he trotted back to the water's edge and began to drink.

Sonja turned to Merlyn. "You didn't want to go golfing?"

"It's not my sport."

"It's never too late to learn."

Merlyn shook her head. Even if she had the money, there was no way.

Sonja smiled. "Well, it's not everyone's cup of tea." She cleared her throat. "So what do you think of Paige now that you've had a chance to be around her for a little while?"

Merlyn had known this question was coming. It was the price of admission. How could she say she didn't think this wedding should happen? She took a deep breath and plunged ahead. "She was pretty engaged at breakfast, talking and eating and even laughing, but something doesn't feel right."

"What do you mean?" Sonja asked.

"I've been watching her. She's always been the happy, popular kid, the one everyone wanted to be friends with." Merlyn decided not to mention her self-absorption. "I have no idea why, but I don't see any of that happiness. She's a bride, and it should be pouring off her like water over Niagara Falls. Something's definitely off."

Instead of being distressed like Merlyn expected, Sonja seemed relieved. "I knew it. I told James, but he didn't see it. In his eyes, his daughter can do no wrong. Never could. And he likes Drake."

Merlyn nodded. "Everybody likes Drake, but he isn't the issue."

"You're right," Sonja said. "The issue is that this marriage is wrong. I realized it from the beginning of Paige's insane rush to the altar. I didn't know what to do about it then, and I still don't. She's an adult and can marry whomever she wants whenever she wants. I certainly can't stop her."

"Have you tried talking to her about it?"

"Yes, but she won't discuss it with me." Sonja sighed. "James and I could say we don't want any part of what I believe is a mistake, but she'd do it anyway. Questioning her decision like that would only create hard feelings. So we're going along, James happily and me with severe reservations."

As they stood silently for a moment, Merlyn watched a pair of swans gliding gracefully across the water some distance away. She knew they were paddling briskly under the water, but they appeared to float effortlessly.

· Like Paige glided across the surface of her life. For all the years Merlyn had known Paige, she was the golden girl floating untroubled through life, the rich kid, the social leader, the self-absorbed girl who wasn't mean as much as unaware. Was that only image? Had Paige always been paddling wildly under the surface, struggling to stay afloat? Or was this mad paddling a recent thing? Merlyn suspected it was the latter.

Sonja patted Merlyn's arm. "Thanks for confirming my feelings.

Now we need to figure out what to do in the next three days to prevent a catastrophe." With those ominous words, she called to Locky, and they walked away.

Winston stood, stretched, and headed back to the inn.

Alone once again, Merlyn continued to watch the swans. Instead of using the majestic birds to analyze Paige, how about herself? If they could give the impression they didn't have to work at gliding, then she could give the impression that dealing with all the betrayals in her life wasn't forcing her to paddle like crazy. Serene and graceful. An ugly duckling turned beautiful swan. That would be her from now on.

Merlyn wished for a pair of binoculars to watch the swans. She glanced at the shed on the property and wondered if there was a pair inside.

She hurried over to check. Nope. Life vests and water toys. Hmm. Life vests. She eyed the pair of kayaks kept by the inn for the enjoyment of guests, then scanned the smooth blue water and grinned. Let the swans glide. She was going to go gliding too.

Merlyn buckled on a red life vest and adjusted it for a comfortable fit—or as comfortable as possible. As much as she disliked the restrictive feel of the vest, she wasn't kayaking by herself without wearing a flotation device. She might be poor and jobless, but she wasn't reckless.

She dragged the red kayak to the dock and lowered it into the water.

Suddenly both Winston and Locky were on the dock with her, curious about what she was doing. Locky seemed ready to jump in again and check out the kayak up close. She could only imagine what kind of disaster that would become.

"No, Locky. Stay," Merlyn told him. "You too, Winston. Sit."

Both dogs plopped their posteriors on the dock.

"Good boys," she crooned. "Now stay."

She studied her kayak. She'd never been on one before, but people kayaked in white water. If they could do that, she could manage the smooth surface of Lake Haven.

The kayak she was going to use was the sit-on-top style rather than the sit-in style, and it was nice and wide for stability. If it had been the other kind, she wouldn't try it alone. With this one, if something went wrong, she'd simply fall off. She'd get wet, but she wouldn't drown trapped upside down.

Merlyn lowered herself carefully onto the seat and smiled with satisfaction when she didn't tip the kayak and fall into the water. She pushed gently away from the dock and began the rhythmic left-right-left-right dip of the paddle. The kayak slid silently through the water.

The dogs watched her go. Locky barked and again looked ready to jump in and swim after her.

"Sit!" she called over her shoulder. "Stay!"

Locky gave a protesting whine, but he stayed on the dock with Winston.

She lifted her face to the sun, glad she had copied her housemates' example of sunglasses and sunscreen. The bill of her Clemson baseball cap helped with the glare too.

Silence folded around Merlyn, and the tension she'd been holding since breakfast floated away like the ripples her paddle made on the water. She moved parallel to the shore and was delighted when she came upon a blue heron.

The bird stood perfectly still as it stared at the lake. Suddenly it stretched its long neck and stabbed into the water. In a flash, it threw its head back and swallowed the hapless fish caught in its beak.

She had only seen such things in nature films before. Trailer girls didn't get to take vacations on lakes. Would Paige, Sue Ann, or Hailey even notice the heron? Ashley would. Ashley noticed everything.

After ten minutes of paddling, Merlyn rotated her shoulders.

They were getting tired from their unaccustomed workout, and she still had to paddle back to the inn. It was time to turn around. She paddled with only one hand, and the boat swung about. As she turned the kayak, the swans floated into view.

Merlyn dug into the water and paddled their way. Swans were another of the many things she'd seen only in movies or on TV, and she wanted to see them close-up. But not too close. She didn't want to upset them. They could be very aggressive—she'd seen some videos online—and she didn't want to have a race with an angry swan. The swan would probably win.

As she neared the birds, she noticed there were four cygnets floating beside the mature swans. The fluffy young swans were adorable, ranging in color from light gray to white. She stopped paddling and watched, entranced. As she did, one mature swan changed her position slightly, and Merlyn realized she had a cygnet on her back. Or his back. She had no idea how to determine the gender of a swan. Or how the five cygnets determined which one got a ride on Mom's—or Pop's—back. The whole family ignored her.

She was so caught up in enjoying the swans that she was unaware of the speedboat bearing down on them until it drew close. Too close and too fast. There were several speedboats on the water, pulling water-skiers or big puffy floats with shrieking kids inside. They were all staying considerably away from the birds. With a lake so huge, there was no need to bother the wildlife. But the boat coming her way seemed intent on doing just that.

Merlyn raised her paddle and waved it in the air. "Go away!" She knew the people on the boat couldn't hear her over the noise of the motor, but shouting at them was automatic. "Slow down and go away!"

Instead, the boat seemed to speed up, and it continued coming right at her and the swans.

Merlyn's heart began to pound, and her hands became slippery on the paddle. Surely whoever was driving saw her and the birds. The swans were bright white against the blue of the water, and she was wearing a red life vest and sitting on a red kayak.

She glanced at the swans. The adults had moved beside each other with the cygnets behind them. A couple more of the little guys had jumped onto their parents' backs. The adults could neither fly away nor paddle to safety because the cygnets weren't old enough to do either.

She turned back to the speedboat and gasped. If it didn't turn, it was going to ram right into her. There was no time to maneuver out of its path. She couldn't try to escape anyway because she froze.

The only thing working was her mind, which ran on a continuous loop. *Don't let it hurt too much. Don't let it hurt too much. Don't let it hurt too much!*

13

Merlyn

At the very last moment the speedboat swerved, throwing up a great spray of water and creating a good-size wave in its wake. The teens on board laughed and cheered their captain as they sped past, then took off to find their next victim.

As the wave hit the kayak broadside, Merlyn knew she was going into the lake. Thank goodness for her life vest. She assumed being thrown in this way wouldn't hurt at all, especially compared to her previous vision of being run over by the speedboat.

Sure enough, the kayak rolled, throwing her off in a tangle of arms and legs. She watched her paddle sail over the swans and disappear right before the water swallowed her.

Merlyn sank despite the life vest. *Up*, she ordered herself. *Up! Follow the bubbles!*

She wasn't a strong swimmer, because swimming lessons were another thing trailer kids didn't get to experience. Rather than feeling at ease in the water, she felt awkward and unsure. In addition, sitting at a desk all day designing websites didn't make her particularly fit.

As Merlyn kicked and flailed with little grace, she started to rise, the life vest helping her. She urged herself to go faster, afraid she was going to run out of breath at any second. *As soon as I have money again*, she vowed, *I'm taking swimming lessons even if I'm the only one in the class older than five.*

Merlyn burst into the air and sucked in huge gulps. For a moment she stayed there, panting and trying to convince herself she wasn't going to drown. She was not in danger, and she would not be frightened. She had merely experienced a momentary dunking. A rescuer would come and save her. Someone must have witnessed the boat upending her.

But it seemed no one had because no one came. Getting herself back to the inn was her only choice. While she tried to decide the best way to accomplish that task, she bobbed in the water, her legs dangling down unprotected.

What kind of creatures lurked in a lake? Merlyn stared into the impenetrable depths. Alligators? Sharks? Not sharks. They were saltwater predators. But alligators weren't. Water moccasins weren't. What about big fish? Or large turtles? She could practically feel a snapping turtle taking off her toes.

She would be safe on top of the kayak. She spun wildly in a circle, searching for it.

Nearby the swans bobbed calmly on the swells, glancing at her without interest. None of them appeared harmed, thank goodness. Sadly, they were probably used to being harassed by foolish bullies who thought getting the best of a bird was something to be proud of.

There was the kayak, upside down and bobbing as calmly as the swans. Merlyn dog-paddled to it and grabbed hold. She felt much more secure with something to hang on to, but she still half-expected something to seize her legs and yank her underwater.

She studied the kayak. How was she supposed to turn it over with no leverage? And how could she get back on it with nothing to push against?

From down at water level, the shore appeared miles away. How would she ever get back there? Even if she could figure out how to get on the kayak, she didn't know where her paddle had gone. She'd have to rest on her stomach and use her hands to scoop water, sort of like a surfer on her board.

A dog that looked as small as one of those little china statuettes in a gift shop ran back and forth on the shore.

Was it Locky? Maybe he'd act like Lassie and get his owners, tell them that she needed rescuing. *Talk about a ridiculous idea.*

Merlyn turned her attention back to something she could control. Or try to. Maybe she could hold on to the kayak and kick herself to shore. With any luck, she'd make it back in time for the wedding. Her skin would be rather wrinkled by then, but if she wore the ruffled dress, it would attract so much horrified attention that no one would notice she resembled a shar-pei.

No, Merlyn needed a better plan than three days in the water. She had to flip the kayak and get back on it. She examined it without any real insight as to the best way to accomplish that, so she tried the first thing that came to mind. She lifted the side closest to her out of the water and pushed so it would go up and over. All that happened was that she sank and the kayak slapped back on the water, still upside down.

When Merlyn surfaced, she sputtered and glared at the kayak.

A thought struck. She didn't have to flip the awkward thing, did she? Couldn't she simply sit on the underside, now exposed to the sun, and paddle? It was slightly curved like a very small sand dune and had a channel running down each side dividing the bottom into thirds. It would make easy sitting. All she needed was her paddle. She scanned the area for it without success.

But first things first. She had to get on the kayak. Then she could search for the paddle because she'd be higher. Once Merlyn located it, she could make her way over to it by scooping water with her hands. Assuming she didn't encounter the lunatics who had flipped her, she could paddle home.

Clutching the fat rim of the boat, she threw one leg onto the hull. Was it a hull? Did kayaks call their bottoms hulls? Who cared? All she wanted was to get her heel into the channel that ran the length of the kayak's bottom.

Merlyn couldn't quite reach. If only she had Sue Ann's long legs instead of her own short ones. Despite her height disadvantage, she somehow had to get the rest of herself up there on the hull with her leg.

She stayed in her strange aquatic split for a few moments as she tried to figure out what to grab hold of for leverage. Unfortunately, the kayak was too wide for her to grip the far side and pull herself up. The width she'd appreciated for extra stability was now a problem. She lowered her leg, which was starting to cramp.

Then Merlyn tried to jump up and onto the kayak by pulling her legs into a crouch and then pushing off. All that happened was that her legs sank. The rest of her remained in exactly the same place. Still, she tried again and again.

Exhausted, she rested her head against the kayak. Merlyn was panting from her useless efforts, and her arms were so heavy. She was starting to get really scared. Maybe she wasn't going to get out of here. What did it feel like to drown?

A drowned bridesmaid would definitely put a damper on the wedding. On the bright side, maybe they'd postpone the ceremony out of respect, and in the meantime, Paige might come to her senses. Sonja would thank Merlyn posthumously for saving Paige. Sue Ann and Hailey would probably cheer her demise, but the others would be sad. She hoped. At least a little bit. She pictured Quint with a devastated expression, and she immediately felt better.

Her hand slipped off the kayak, and she gasped in surprise as she went underwater. All it took was a quick kick in combination with the buoyancy of the life vest, and she was back at the surface, coughing and sputtering and trying to catch her breath. Her nose and lungs burned from the water she'd swallowed.

Merlyn fumbled for the kayak, but it wasn't where she'd left it. It had been pushed by the little waves she'd made as she flopped around. Even though it was only a few feet away, she was so weary that it seemed like miles.

She'd seen a movie once about a woman who went scuba diving and got lost at sea. The woman became so weary and hopeless that she finally let herself sink. Merlyn had never understood such an action. Surely you should continue fighting for as long as you could breathe.

Now she understood. She was scared and tired and certain no one would come for her. If she was this frightened in a nice civilized lake, what would it be like to be lost in the vastness of the ocean?

Please, God, help! Get me out of here!

Merlyn took a determined breath now that she could finally breathe without coughing. Then she paddled to the kayak with leaden arms. She made her fingers like claws as she grabbed the little channel that ran the length of the boat's bottom.

The irony of her situation struck her. She was in danger of drowning within sight of shore. If she knew how to swim, she could swim to shore and save herself. But she couldn't swim. If she knew how to get back on the kayak, she could paddle to shore, even if the paddle had to be her hands. But she didn't know how to get back on.

She had only one choice. *Hold on!*

Grace

Grace was catching up on some bookkeeping when Winston dashed into her private living room, barked once, and ran out.

She smiled. She couldn't help it. The little shih tzu mix was so cute. The bark-and-run trick was new, though. They'd have to talk about it because he really couldn't run around barking. The guests would not appreciate the noise.

He rushed into the room and barked again.

This time Winnie followed him, taking care to step around him. "What's gotten into Winston?"

"I have no idea." Grace put a finger to her lips. "Hush, young man. No barking in the house."

Winston turned and ran out of the room. He stopped in the hallway and glanced over his shoulder at Grace. When she didn't follow, the dog stared at her and barked once more.

Grace frowned. Why was her dog so agitated?

"What's that, Lassie? Timmy fell down the well?" Winnie laughed. "I used to love that show. Lassie was such a pretty dog."

"She was. Or rather, the male dogs that portrayed her were," Grace said absently as she stood up. "I think we're safe in saying it's not Timmy trapped in a well, but something's going on."

Winston spun in a circle, gave another little bark, and flew down the hall.

Feeling a bit foolish, Grace followed him with Winnie right behind her. Winston was a dog above all dogs, but did she really think he was having a Lassie moment trying to get her to help?

But what if he was? She couldn't ignore him in case someone truly needed help.

Winston led them to the back door. As soon as Grace opened it, he rushed outside toward the lake.

As Grace continued to follow Winston, she noticed the Repperts' dreadlocked dog across the lawn. He barked as he ran back and forth along the lake's edge with detours onto the dock.

"That's one interesting dog," Winnie said, watching Locky.

"He's a puli." Grace scanned the water. "There, by the swans! See it?"

"What?" Winnie shaded her eyes with her hand. "You mean that blob of red?"

Grace hurried inside the inn to retrieve her binoculars. She needed to check that red. Someone in danger on the lake was a constant possibility, and Grace went cold at the thought. And time would be critical.

She ran back outside and across the lawn to rejoin Winnie.

When Locky spotted them, he sprinted over to Grace and Winnie and herded them toward the dock. They went willingly.

As Grace put the binoculars to her eyes, Sonja and James jogged across the lawn.

"I told you it was Locky I heard." Sonja ran a hand through her hair. "Something is wrong."

Locky and Winston ran around the dock and barked, their gazes fixed on the lake.

James squinted as he studied the water. "What's got the dogs so worked up?"

"There may be a swimmer in distress," Winnie replied.

Grace found the swans through the binoculars and slowly scanned the water around them. Her heart was pounding and not from her run. Every minute counted when dealing with a catastrophe on the water. Drowning always lurked, ready to pounce on the weary and the untrained.

Once she'd called 911 over an upended sailboat. At first, she hadn't seen the sailor, but even as she and the dispatcher talked, a head appeared. The man had grabbed the keel and pulled himself onto the bottom of the boat, where he stood waving his hands to attract help.

Right now, the sun shone fiercely on the water, making it difficult to see, but the red was definitely there. Was that a head? It was hard to tell.

Grace lowered the binoculars and removed her cell phone from her pocket. From the corner of her eye she saw the kayaks—or the orange kayak, singular. The red one was missing.

She punched in 911 and listened to the ring at the other end. She raised the binoculars again. Now that she knew what she was searching for, she was able to interpret what she saw. The red was definitely one of the inn's kayaks.

"This is 911. What's your emergency?"

"An upended kayak about a half mile offshore," Grace answered. "I haven't located the person using it yet."

"Do you know who it is?" Sonja asked.

Grace suspected it was Merlyn because the rest of the bridal party was golfing. She held up a finger as she talked with the dispatcher, giving her all the information she had. She hung up and dialed Spencer Lewis.

When he answered, Grace immediately relaxed. She was so glad he was home. "One of our kayaks is floating out on the lake, and I can't see the young woman using it," she said without preamble.

"I'll be right there," Spencer answered, then clicked off.

No fuss, no questions, just action. Grace could picture him running across the lawn to his dock and speeding to Merlyn. He was such a good guy.

Sonja gave Grace a questioning look.

"Spencer's a good friend," Grace explained. "His Blossom Hill Farm is right down the road, and he has a small motorboat moored at his dock."

"Two boats on the way," Winnie said. "What a relief."

Grace returned her phone to her pocket and peered through the binoculars again. The kayak had moved slightly, and this time she was sure she spotted a head. "I see her!" The relief she felt made her dizzy.

"Who is it?" Sonja asked.

"I think it's Merlyn," Grace said.

Sonja sank into a chair as if her knees had given out.

"Quint's on his way." James slid his phone into the holder clipped to his belt. "He's out fishing and is probably the closest."

The four of them stared at the small head bobbing in the big lake. All they could do was wait and pray that help arrived in time.

15

Merlyn

Another speedboat headed toward her. Merlyn turned her head to protect herself from the wave it would kick up. If she could help it, she did not want to go underwater again. She was afraid that one of these times, she wouldn't be able to kick back to the surface and breathe in life-giving air.

Merlyn gripped the kayak's underside channel as hard as she could, which wasn't very hard because the indentations were shallow and there was nothing to wrap her fingers around.

The boat slowed at the last moment and reached her with hardly a ripple on the surface of the water.

When she glanced up, she was surprised to see Quint.

He grinned at her. "Can I give you a lift?"

Merlyn couldn't believe she was saved. She started to cry.

Quint didn't roll his eyes or laugh at her. He simply asked, "Can you paddle around to the back of the boat where the ladder is?"

She nodded, feeling foolish about the tears but unable to stop them. It wasn't the best way to impress a nice guy, but his grin and kindness after all the smirks and unkindness of the past months broke something inside her. When she gave a little kick, the kayak bumped the side of Quint's boat.

"You're going to have to let go of the kayak," Quint said, again with no censure.

The thought of letting go of the kayak terrified her. Tired as she was, it'd be straight to the bottom if she let go. Her distress must have shown on her face because the next thing she knew, Quint jumped into the water beside her.

In disbelief, Merlyn gazed into his handsome face. "You're getting all wet," she said, stating the obvious.

He shrugged. "I'll dry. Come on. Let go and hold on to me."

She tried to release her grip, but her fingers felt welded to the kayak.

Quint must have seen her white knuckles because he rested a hand over hers. "Relax. I've got you. Just hold on to me."

His hand felt warm and strong, and tears stung her eyes again. "You'll sink. I'll sink you."

"No, that won't happen. I promise." He held out an arm. "Hold on and kick. It's only a few feet to the back of the boat. We'll make the trip together."

Merlyn stared at his muscular arm that appeared strong enough to support her. *Grab it,* she ordered. Instead, she launched herself at him and wrapped her arms around his neck. If his arm was strong enough to support her, his whole body had to be better. She held her breath, waiting for them to go under.

But Quint didn't sink. He didn't even flinch.

"Whatever works for you." He tapped her arm. "But not so tight, okay? I like to breathe."

She loosened her hold.

Quint moved through the water with ease and stopped beside the ladder that reflected silver in the sunshine. "Grab on."

Merlyn put out one arm and seized the ladder. Her other arm still strangled him.

He pointed to the ladder. "Other hand."

She didn't want to let go of him. He was her safe place. Reluctantly, she clutched the ladder with her other hand.

"Hold tight," Quint instructed.

Merlyn nodded. She wouldn't let anyone pry her fingers from the ladder.

Then he sank. Just disappeared.

"Quint!" she yelled, staring down into the dark water.

He surfaced beside her. "Right here. Now up you go." He put his hands on her waist and gave her a boost.

Merlyn climbed the ladder and into the boat on shaky legs, then collapsed into the passenger seat.

Quint followed her on board. "You're safe now. You did well."

Sure she had. She'd almost drowned, and she'd almost choked him when he came to rescue her. The tears started again, much to her embarrassment. With the exception of the last few months, she wasn't usually a crier. Growing up had taken too much energy to waste on something as useless as crying. She tried to get herself under control.

Quint held out an oversize towel that had seen better days. "Dry your face, and then drape it around you."

Merlyn took it gratefully and buried her face in its shaggy depths, mopping up both the lake residue and the tears. She flapped it open and wrapped it around her shoulders. To her surprise, she realized she was shaking with chill.

A boat eased in beside them. A man with salt-and-pepper hair called out, "I'm Spencer Lewis, a friend of Grace Porter. Everything all right here?"

Quint waved. "I've got her. She's fine."

"Good. I'll tell Grace all's well. See you." Spencer motored off, his phone to his ear.

Another boat with the word *Police* emblazoned on its side pulled up. "You folks okay?" called an officer wearing reflective sunglasses.

As the officer turned his head to check the boat and its occupants,

Merlyn got a distorted glimpse of herself in his sunglasses. A drenched poodle came to mind.

Quint talked to the officer and thanked him.

When the police boat pulled away, Quint grinned at her. "Three potential rescuers. You're a very popular lady."

She snorted. "Hardly. Ask anyone."

He ignored her statement and lifted his cell phone from the cup holder on the boat's dashboard. "Got her," he told some unknown person. "She's fine if a bit waterlogged. We'll be there shortly."

Merlyn was so tired that she didn't even care where he was taking her.

Quint stuck his phone back into the cup holder. "Let's rescue your kayak."

"It's not mine." As soon as she said it, she cringed. She knew her brain was indeed waterlogged if she made such a foolish comment.

"So you stole it?" he asked as he manipulated the boat close to the wandering kayak. "I've never met a more intriguing thief."

Merlyn turned red at his compliment, but the blush warmed her, and her shaking stopped. Of course, it could have been the combined warmth of the sun and the towel that eased her chill, but she didn't think so. "If I was a thief, I'd be a pretty unsuccessful one. It belongs to the inn."

Putting his boat in neutral, Quint leaned over the side and effortlessly hauled the kayak on board. "Now where's the paddle?"

Merlyn stood on wobbly legs and clutched the back of the seat for support as she scanned the area. "It was by the swans, but I think they've drifted away since I fell in."

"There it is." Quint motored to the paddle, retrieved it, and set it on the bottom of the boat beside the kayak.

She sank to her seat and told herself it would be impolite to fall asleep. It would be only a few minutes to shore, and then she could sleep in her room if her legs would support her as she climbed that curving staircase that suddenly loomed as large as Mount Kilimanjaro.

Quint tied up to the dock at the inn, where a welcoming party waited for them.

Merlyn forced herself to smile. She was rewarded for her effort by watching all the faces lose their anxious expressions and smile back.

James held out his hand to help her out of the boat. Quint steadied her from behind as she climbed onto the shore.

When Merlyn felt less dizzy and could be sure her words came out right, she would have to compliment Sonja on the good manners of the men in her family.

Grace pulled the wet towel from Merlyn's shoulders and draped her in a fluffy blue one that could have wrapped around her twice. She handed another towel to Quint, who slung it around his neck.

Merlyn clasped her towel close. "Quint rescued your kayak."

"That was very kind of him." Grace smiled at Quint, then turned back to Merlyn. "But I can buy another kayak. We were more concerned about irreplaceable you."

Merlyn smiled weakly, feeling overwhelmed by the attention.

"Let's get her inside so she can sit down." Quint put an arm around Merlyn's shoulders and started guiding her toward the inn.

As the group moved across the lawn, a car came up the front drive and pulled into the parking area. Paige, Ashley, Sue Ann, and Hailey climbed out and stared at them as they approached the inn.

Merlyn tried to move away from Quint, but he held her fast. "They'll—" she protested.

"Be their usual catty selves?" he interrupted.

She stared at him in surprise. "Not Paige. Not Ashley."

He nodded. "I've wondered for years why Paige keeps that pair as friends."

"I think it's more that they keep her."

Quint's phone rang, but he made no move to answer.

"Go ahead," Merlyn said. "It might be important."

He checked the screen, then put the phone to his ear. "Hey." He listened a moment. "At the inn where the girls are staying. Come over here." He glanced at Merlyn and smiled. "As a matter of fact, yes, I did go fishing, and you should see what I caught."

Quint disconnected and turned to his mother. "That was Colton. The guys picked up the wedding stuff at the rental shop, and they're bringing it here."

Sonja seemed relieved. "Good. I was worried about you placing long-distance orders. Be sure to try the suits on right away, all of you."

"Yes, Mother," Quint said.

"Did you speak to your superior officers in that sarcastic tone?" Sonja asked, lightly smacking his arm.

"All the time." Quint grinned. "Don't worry. We'll try everything on. I promise."

After they walked into the inn, Paige and the others entered.

Paige and Ashley were all smiles. But Sue Ann and Hailey shot lethal looks that could have slain Merlyn if Quint hadn't stepped in front of her.

16

Ashley

If Ashley had gotten her way, she would have spent the afternoon hiding in her room, but she didn't have that luxury. Everything was planned for the group, and she didn't have the courage to say she needed to be alone. Merlyn had been lucky to escape by herself this morning, even if she had almost drowned.

How did I ever get into this mess?

But she knew. Paige had called and said, "I want you to be in my wedding."

"You're getting married? What a wonderful surprise! I'd love to."

With any luck, Ashley would be calling Paige to be in her own wedding in a few months. Things were going so well, even though she hadn't seen him recently. She'd e-mailed and texted a couple of times and he hadn't responded, but he was a busy man in line for the sales manager job at the car dealership.

"I know it seems quick," Paige said, "but I've known him forever."

"Who is he?" Ashley asked. Growing up in the same town, they knew many of the same people, though their paths had diverged after high school. Paige was one of the few people Ashley had stayed close to, courtesy of social media.

"Drake Fremont."

Ashley blinked. She couldn't have heard right. "Who?"

"Drake Fremont," Paige repeated. "You know him. He's friends with Quint and Colton."

Ashley couldn't breathe. She couldn't speak.

"I know it's a bit fast," Paige continued. "But I'm so happy."

It was only later that Ashley remembered the lack of happiness in Paige's voice. At the time, the drumming in her ears drowned out all thought.

And so here she was, trying to make it through an event she would never have committed to if she'd known the groom's name from the beginning.

The guys had brought pizza, and the whole group ate lunch on the back veranda. Paige sat next to Drake, and his sandy head dipped to her shiny one as they frequently murmured to each other despite the general conversation swirling around them.

Probably bride and groom stuff. What did Ashley expect? Except there was something in their manner that nagged at her, and it wasn't caused by her unrequited love. Where were the goofy grins between sweethearts? The touching? The loving gazes?

She'd been in other weddings, and she knew what a bride and groom should act like a few days before their wedding. Paige and Drake seemed more like friends having a nice conversation than a man and a woman in love.

Drake glanced up and caught her watching him.

Ashley quickly turned away, pretending she was interested in what PJ and Colton were talking about, whatever that was, but not before she saw Drake's concerned expression.

She made her face serene even as she swallowed angry tears. Drake didn't have the right to be concerned about her. The minute he slid that engagement ring onto Paige's finger, he'd forfeited that privilege.

Ashley couldn't believe he'd done this to her. It felt completely out of character. He wasn't a guy given to deceit. At least she hadn't thought so. He was open and honest when they'd been dating. He'd begun driving to Charlotte every weekend to see her. She knew he liked her. What she hadn't known was that he must have been seeing Paige too. What else could explain his falling for her with such an earthshaking thud?

She wished she could despise him for two-timing her, but he'd made no commitment to her. He should have. She'd be a much better wife for him than Paige. Drake was too nice for a strong personality like hers. Didn't he realize Paige would run him over and then resent him for not being strong? He needed Ashley's softer manner and gentler spirit. She would love him the way he deserved to be loved if only she had a chance.

When PJ and Colton laughed, Ashley forced a laugh too and even managed to swallow a slice of pizza. She washed it down her dry throat with the sweet iced tea the inn provided. Charlotte's brownies and cookies smelled heavenly, but they were more than she could handle right now.

Ashley was once again wondering how she could sneak away and get to her room without anyone noticing she was gone when Quint stood up, more or less signaling lunch was over.

Quint grinned at Merlyn. "Get your suit on. I'm teaching you to water-ski."

Merlyn appeared less than thrilled at the prospect. "I think I've had enough of the water today."

Hailey clapped. "What a great idea, Quint." She pointedly ignored the fact that Quint had asked Merlyn, not her, to go.

Didn't Hailey understand that Quint was taken with Merlyn? Or did she get it and had decided to fight back? Not that Ashley thought it would do any good. She almost felt sorry for Hailey with her unrequited love. Ashley knew how much it hurt.

A little later when everyone gathered on the dock, Hailey was the first to buckle her life vest. "All ready, Quint," she called.

He nodded and stepped into his boat.

Hailey slid into the deeper water at the end of the dock, and Colton handed the skis down to her.

"I need someone to be the spotter." Quint turned to Merlyn. "Interested?"

Hailey spun to stare at him in disbelief.

Ashley bit back a smile. *Foiled again.*

Merlyn, lovely in a sleek black swimsuit, walked to the boat. "What does a spotter do?"

Hailey snorted. She might as well have said, "You don't know what a spotter does? What an idiot." If she was trying to impress Quint, she was going about it all wrong.

Quint ignored Hailey and spoke to Merlyn. "The spotter is the person who watches the skier and tells the driver if she falls."

"All I have to do is watch and yell if someone falls?" Merlyn smiled. "I can do that." She took his hand and stepped into the boat. He escorted her to a back-facing seat.

Ashley watched Hailey to see her reaction, but for once she was wise enough to busy herself slipping on the skis as if she didn't see the attention Quint was paying Merlyn.

Quint took his boat in an arc, looping back to idle a few feet in front of Hailey. He secured one end of the towline to the back of the boat and tossed the other end to her.

Hailey caught it and grasped the handle, settling the line between her ski tips. "Ready!"

Quint drove slowly forward until the line was taut.

"Go!" Hailey yelled.

Quint gunned the motor, and Hailey rose from the water with perfect form, knees bent, arms straight, body leaning slightly back. He took her on a long ride since it was obvious that she had stamina and skill.

When they returned, Quint circled toward the dock, and at just the right moment Hailey dropped the towline. She almost floated into the shallow water, where she touched bottom and stepped from her skis.

If she hadn't looked so proud of herself, Ashley would have felt more like joining the applause.

Then several of the guys skied. Colton was the best, but Drake was pretty good as he glided back and forth through the boat's wake.

Reynolds skied on one ski, then tried to ski barefoot.

When he went down with a big splash, Sue Ann rose from her seat and clapped. "Way to go, babe!"

Merlyn let Quint know Reynolds was down, and the boat circled to pick him up.

Reynolds climbed the back ladder, and Merlyn handed him a towel. He basically ignored her, turning toward the others and raising his hands in a triumphant gesture.

Quint patted the passenger seat beside him, and Merlyn sat there. Reynolds sprawled in the boat's rear seats as Quint collected the bobbing ski and brought the boat back to the dock.

"Your turn, Merlyn," Hailey called with a definite barb in her voice.

Merlyn turned to Quint. It was obvious she didn't want to give it a try with everyone watching.

Quint, nice guy that he was, evidently understood. He shook his head. "No more skiing this afternoon. I'm low on gas. I need enough to get to the marina to fill up." He stepped from the boat and extended a hand to help Merlyn out.

Paige rose from the lounge she'd been sunning on. "I'm going up to take a shower and rest. I've had more than enough sun for one day. I don't want a red and peeling nose for the wedding photos."

Not that Paige's nose would ever be so impolite as to peel, but her move started a small stampede back to the inn.

Ashley had to smile when she heard Quint ask Merlyn, "Want to try skiing with your audience gone?"

Merlyn raised her brow. "I thought you didn't have enough gas for more skiing."

"So I prevaricated to save your tender sensibilities," Quint said, grinning.

She laughed. "Your vocabulary is very impressive."

"We Navy men are all impressive."

"And modest," Merlyn teased.

"That too," Quint agreed. "Ride to the marina with me?"

Merlyn's smile was full of delight as she took Quint's hand and stepped back into the boat.

Ashley sighed as she watched the two of them together. *Bittersweet.* That word defined the conflicting emotions the budding romance aroused in her. She was glad for Merlyn, who deserved so much better than what she had been dealt, but it hurt that Ashley's own sweet dreams had gone up in smoke.

She folded a couple of chairs that had been left on the dock and turned to take them to the storage shed, then hesitated when she saw Drake standing by the shed watching her. As Ashley carried the chairs over there, she straightened her spine and acted as if his presence was no concern of hers.

Without a word, Drake took the chairs from her. She made sure their hands didn't touch. He put the chairs neatly away in the shed.

"Thanks," Ashley muttered. She went back to the dock to retrieve her towel and canvas bag.

Drake trailed her and grabbed a towel of his own.

She ignored him and started crossing the lawn.

He fell into step beside her. "How are you doing?"

Ashley glanced at him, trying to figure out what he meant. Was he asking a casual question he might ask anyone? Or was he concerned about her because he knew he'd hurt her? *Kill me now if it's the latter.* "I'm fine. Just fine." Her voice had an edge to it, but she didn't care. He could make of it what he would.

Drake nodded. "That's good."

Her stride faltered. Did he really think she was fine? Was he that dense?

"I'm sorry, you know." He sounded so sincere that she wanted to slug him.

"You are?" she asked. "About what?"

"Things. The way everything turned out."

"You're sorry about things," Ashley said.

"Yeah, I am."

"What things?" She stopped walking and glared at him. "Tell me, would you? What things?"

Drake stopped too. He appeared uncomfortable as he gestured vaguely to the inn. "All this."

"All this what?" Ashley persisted. He was driving her nuts and breaking her heart at the same time. Just as he'd been doing for months.

"The wedding and all."

"You're sorry about your wedding?" she echoed.

He nodded. "And all."

"Did it ever occur to you that if you're sorry about your wedding, maybe you shouldn't be getting married?"

Drake frowned at her. "That wasn't what I meant, and you know it."

Was that a trace of temper in his voice? Well, Ashley could do anger too. "You don't owe the Repperts your soul," she hissed.

His head snapped back as if she'd slapped him. "What did you say?"

"I think you're paying them back for their kindness all those years ago by marrying Paige." There. She'd finally said it.

"You don't know what you're talking about," Drake replied.

"They helped you because they're nice, not because they wanted you beholden to them forever," Ashley said. "Do you think they want you making choices that will ruin your life and Paige's? And all out of some warped feeling of obligation?"

"You think I'm getting married out of obligation?" he asked sharply.

Her anger gave way to uncertainty. Maybe she was wrong. Maybe Drake loved Paige. What did she really know? She was just a lost, lonely, heartbroken woman trying to understand what had happened to her life.

"I'd appreciate it if you'd stop trying to analyze Paige and me." Drake's voice was cold enough to give her a chill in spite of the heat. "Tell me this. You think you've figured out why I'm marrying her, but why do you think she's marrying me? Could it be possible that she wants to marry me?"

Ashley had no trouble thinking Paige might want to marry Drake. Any woman in her right mind would want to marry him. He was an amazing man. But that didn't mean just any woman was right for him, even someone as special as Paige. Why didn't he understand that? His obtuseness made her want to scream.

"You want to know something?" Ashley almost stamped her foot in frustration, but she caught herself in time to save at least a shred of her dignity. "It makes me unbelievably sad that I won't get what I want. It would have been good. It would have been wonderful."

She marched away, praying her shaking legs would support her long enough to reach her room, where she could collapse in a blubbering heap.

Merlyn

Wednesday night the group went to a small dinner theater with delicious food and an exciting play that involved some audience participation. Paige was selected to swoon over the leading man, and she handled her three lines with spirit, drawing loud cheers from their party. Colton was stabbed at the end of the first act and died with style. Again, their group cheered mightily. Merlyn enjoyed the chance to laugh, a rare event these days.

Later that night when she fell into bed, she slept deeply and woke refreshed. She didn't get up right away, luxuriating in the comfortable bed.

Then Merlyn remembered the plans for Thursday. Ever since her arrival when she'd read the schedule, she had been dreading the day's venue.

Shopping at the outlet mall.

Why would she want to go shopping when she had no money? Perusing enticing things with no possibility of buying even one of them was as exciting as Christmas with no presents, Easter with no basket of goodies, or Halloween with no candy. Unfortunately, there was no getting out of the trip. She'd managed to avoid going golfing, but she couldn't beg off another planned activity.

Forcing a positive attitude, Merlyn got ready and joined the others downstairs. When they arrived at the mall, she was relieved as they split up into two groups. Merlyn and Ashley had a good time window-shopping and talking. Later, they met the others for lunch, and Merlyn endured Hailey's and Sue Ann's conspicuous consumption and compulsive show-and-tell. At least the food was tasty.

Back at the inn, Merlyn savored the chance to sit in the late afternoon sun on the inn's dock and relax.

Everyone went into Magnolia Harbor for dinner. Wearing a teal-and-white dress that always made her feel elegant, Merlyn climbed out of Quint's car at Turner's Lakeside Grill. As she grabbed her white sweater in case it was chilly inside the restaurant, she heard Sonja call to her. Quint followed Merlyn, and they joined his mother.

"We've reserved three tables for our group," Sonja told them. "James and I would like it if you two joined us."

Merlyn hoped her surprise wasn't too obvious, but her smile was genuine. She glanced at Quint, who nodded. "That would be lovely. Thank you."

Hailey overheard and scowled, undermining the picture of a charming Southern belle she evidently meant to project. She wouldn't say anything snarky about the invitation while Sonja was around, but maybe she would make a snide comment to Merlyn later.

In an attempt to forestall her attack, Merlyn smiled sweetly at Hailey. "I love your dress. You look beautiful tonight."

Hailey regarded her with a slight frown as she apparently searched for an insult in Merlyn's comment. When she didn't find one, she seemed confused.

Colton appeared at Hailey's side. "Come on. We'll sit with these two." He motioned toward Ashley and PJ.

Hailey forced a smile. "Sure. Why not?" She obviously knew she had no other choice.

Colton took Hailey's elbow and guided her over to their tablemates.

Right before the hostess escorted that foursome to their table,

Colton glanced back over his shoulder. He widened his eyes at Quint, then winked at Merlyn.

She laughed. "Taking one for the team, is he?"

Quint sighed in mock resignation. "I'll spend the rest of my life working off the favors I owe him for this week."

Merlyn was nervous when the hostess ushered them to their table and she took her seat. Sonja and James were formidable, no matter how kind they had been thus far. Being asked to sit with them was like being called to the principal's office. Her imagination created all sorts of harrowing scenarios.

She told herself to relax. Though she couldn't quite manage that, she was able to enjoy watching Quint and his parents together. The affection and respect they had for each other made her smile even as it pricked her heart. What they shared was everything she had always longed for with her mother. Not that her mother didn't love her. She did in her own dysfunctional way. And she had tried. Sometimes she had even succeeded, like with the outfit for that fateful birthday party.

The waitress arrived for their drink orders.

"Would you like a glass of wine with your dinner?" James asked Merlyn. "Red? White? Rosé?"

"No thanks," Merlyn answered. "I'll have a sweetened iced tea, please." She held her breath as she waited for criticism. Reynolds always considered a glass of wine not merely a social nicety but a social necessity.

"Bring her a glass of what I'm having," he'd tell the server.

"Don't do that," she always said. "I don't drink. I won't drink. Ordering it for me is a waste of money."

"You'll learn to drink. Everyone does," he replied. "You must learn how to behave properly in social situations."

"Like not drinking will make me a social pariah." She'd leave the glass he'd gotten for her untouched beside her plate.

He'd then sulk for half the meal because Merlyn hadn't been grateful for his generous instruction in the art of living. With hindsight, she realized he regarded himself as Professor Henry Higgins to her Eliza Doolittle. Too often it was, "Do this, Merlyn. No, no! Don't do that." It was a wonder he didn't have her singing about the rain in Spain staying mainly in the plain.

Unlike Reynolds, the Repperts didn't seem to care what she drank. No one criticized her for getting iced tea.

The waitress took the rest of the drink orders.

After the waitress left, James turned to Merlyn. "How did you get involved in website design?"

She smiled, flattered he knew what she did. Oh, wait. Of course he knew. Everyone in Reynolds knew, and that wasn't all they knew. Ah, well, there was nothing she could do but face things head-on.

"I majored in Web design in college." *On a full academic scholarship, thank you very much*, Merlyn thought with the usual mix of pride and thanksgiving. "When my friends and I graduated and some of them were striking out on their own, they approached me to design their sites. Free was all they could afford, but it was good experience."

James gave Sonja a reminiscent smile. "I remember those days when we were getting started and prayed for enough income to pay the rent."

Sonja patted his arm. "We ate so much peanut butter and jelly." She made a face. "I still have trouble eating it."

"That never stopped you from giving it to us kids." Quint glanced at Merlyn. "On whole wheat bread. Can you believe it? I didn't know it was supposed to be on squishy white bread until I was in the Navy."

"Poor kid," James said with a notable lack of sympathy.

Merlyn smiled, enjoying the gentle teasing between people who loved each other.

The waitress returned with their drinks, then asked for their dinner orders. Merlyn chose trout almandine, Sonja cedar-plank salmon, and James and Quint New York strip steak. The waitress assured them it would be ready soon and hurried away.

"Are you familiar with Reppert Irrigation?" James asked Merlyn.

"I know it's your company," Merlyn answered. "But beyond that, I confess I don't know much."

"We irrigate everything from golf courses to cemeteries," James replied.

"He owns three public golf courses," Sonja inserted.

James smiled at her. "In partnership."

Sonja shrugged. "They're your babies."

James leaned back. "Recently our company has been doing a lot to bring fresh drinking water to people living in villages in developing countries. But what we've done is only a drop in the great bucket of need, if you'll forgive the pun. We want to do more. We want to organize our participation, send more teams, and encourage others to join us in this important work."

"That's wonderful, Mr. Reppert, and very exciting," Merlyn said. "It's something that can make a huge difference in the lives of those affected."

He held up a finger. "No more Mr. Reppert. Please call me James." He smiled at her, then at Sonja. "James, one syllable."

Merlyn felt her face flush as she laughed and repeated, "James, one syllable."

The conversation paused as a server delivered their meals.

"We want to support teams who will go to needy areas and install springhouses and wells and train people in basic sanitation," James continued. "We want to give them their first bar of soap."

Merlyn tried to imagine never having a bar of soap, but all she could see was the supermarket aisle lined with soaps and detergents and cleaning products.

"To generate the support that we want for this project," James went on, "we need a social media presence and a website."

Merlyn blinked and managed to swallow her mouthful without choking. Was he saying what she thought he was?

James studied her for a moment, and she did her best not to squirm. "I've checked the R&S Design site, which I understand used to be R&M. Some of the sites R&S or R&M developed are clever and innovative, but the more recent ones lack that creative sparkle."

What should Merlyn say? She couldn't announce that she was good at what she did and Sue Ann wasn't. Or that she had that creative sparkle James was talking about and Sue Ann didn't. She cleared her throat. "I haven't seen the site recently, so I can't comment on any recent designs."

That was a true answer. After she'd been kicked out of the company, she compulsively studied the site until she realized they were dismantling the work she'd begun for a big new client. After she started losing sleep over it, she made herself stop checking the site.

Her comment must have been satisfactory because James said, "Would you be interested in working with us? We would like you to design a Water for the World site, develop our social media presence, and post some videos."

Merlyn was thrilled. Inside she was turning cartwheels, jumping up and down, and throwing confetti, but she kept her demeanor calm and professional. "Of course. I'd count it an honor to work with you on such a worthwhile project."

James smiled. "Good. We'll talk more after the wedding. While I'll want to sign off on everything you develop because I'm a nosy old guy, you'll mainly be working with Quint."

She glanced at Quint, surprised.

He grinned at her. "Do you think we can work together?" The twinkle in his eyes set butterflies fluttering in her stomach.

Sonja patted Quint's hand. "He's just become CEO of Water for the World, our nonprofit division."

"We've got great things ahead," James told Merlyn. "I'm glad you'll be joining us."

Merlyn laid her knife and fork neatly across her empty plate. She couldn't believe it. Just like that, she was employed again and with a client she both respected and trusted. It appeared her days in the desert were over.

What she needed now was a really great name for her new company so Reppert Irrigation knew who to pay. Merlyn's Miraculous Media Marvels popped into her mind, and she swallowed a giggle. Marshall Media had a nice ring to it. Whatever name she finally chose, she'd learned a valuable lesson about business from Reynolds. This time she would control everything, both creative and monetary.

Even as Merlyn ordered dessert and coffee, ideas began scrolling through her mind. She glanced at the table where Reynolds and Sue Ann sat. They would be furious when they heard she'd been awarded the Water for the World contract.

She smiled.

Merlyn

As Merlyn and Quint left the restaurant after dinner, she couldn't stop smiling.

Quint cocked an eyebrow at her. "You seem quite pleased with yourself."

"Not with myself." She did a little dance. "With life at the moment. And if you had anything to do with your father's offer, thank you."

"I might have made a suggestion or two," he admitted. "But Mom and Dad had already decided to run the idea by me. So it all worked out."

Colton walked up behind them, Hailey at his side. He glanced from the smiling Merlyn to his brother. "A done deal?"

Quint nodded.

Colton smiled. "Good."

"What's a done deal?" Hailey asked, a note of suspicion in her voice.

Merlyn wanted to shout, "Don't tell!" Anything good for her was something bad to Hailey, and the last thing she wanted was Hailey's evil eye trained on her.

Quint put out a hand as if to stop his brother.

But Colton didn't pick up the warning. "Merlyn's working with us at Water for the World. Website design and all that." He faced Merlyn. "I'm the vice president in charge of recruitment, which means I'm responsible for getting volunteer teams together. I'll work with you on the best ways to use social media to that end."

Merlyn was delighted with Colton's approval even as she worried about Hailey's reaction to the news.

Hailey spun around to gape at Merlyn, then hurried away and fell into step beside Sue Ann.

After a few whispered words, Sue Ann stopped dead. "What?" Her shrill voice cut through the night air.

There was more whispering, and a moment later, Hailey, Sue Ann, and Reynolds were glaring at Merlyn.

Quint opened the car door for her. "Ignore them."

"Easier said than done," she remarked as she climbed into the passenger seat.

Quint walked around the car and got in. "I've noticed their hostility other times. What's their deal? What terrible thing did you do to set them off?" He smiled, letting her know he didn't think there was a terrible thing.

Merlyn shrugged. It felt embarrassing and awkward talking about why people didn't like her with the one person she most wanted to like her.

He started the car and pulled out of the lot. "Let me guess. They're jealous."

She stared at him in astonishment. "You think they're jealous? Of me?"

"Of course," Quint responded. "Sue Ann's worried Reynolds will realize he let the better woman get away."

"I didn't get away," Merlyn protested. "He sent me away."

His grin was visible in the light from the dashboard. "His mistake is my opportunity. As for Hailey, did the hostility start before I showed how interested I was in you?"

"I-interested?" she stammered, feeling heat suffuse her face.

He laughed. "Why the surprise? It's not like I've been hiding it."

"I thought you were just being nice."

"You're not used to that either, are you?" He sobered. "And Hailey probably has a lot to do with it."

"From kindergarten on," she said.

"You're kidding."

"I wish I was. Hailey and Sue Ann have been a thorn in my side my whole life."

Quint furrowed his brow. "My sister isn't like that, is she?"

"No, it's just those two," Merlyn answered. "They've been like guards at the gates of Castle Paige since we were kids, selecting those they thought were good enough to be Paige's friends. Ashley made the cut, but I didn't."

"And Paige let them do that?" he asked.

"I don't think she knew. She's always been nice to me when she was allowed to speak to me. Hailey and Sue Ann are clever. They don't let her see that nasty side of them." Though Merlyn had to admit they were being unusually blatant with their dislike this week. But Paige was too preoccupied with whatever was bothering her to notice.

"I can understand why they decided not to let you in the castle," Quint said. "You're prettier, you're smarter, you're definitely nicer, and you've got genuine talent."

Merlyn blushed. "But both of them are pretty and smart."

"I notice you didn't mention talent. Or niceness."

She smiled.

"I need to add discretion to your list of qualities," Quint said. "So what happened to bring out their nastiness? Originally, I mean."

Merlyn gazed out the window, collecting her thoughts. "The best I can come up with is that I grew up in a trailer park. They decided I wasn't good enough, and nothing has ever changed their minds. Oh, and as I grew up, I had the audacity to rise above my beginnings."

"I hope you're ashamed of yourself for not only surviving but thriving," Quint teased.

"Stricken to my very core."

"I think they should be impressed that you've done so well for yourself. I certainly am."

"Thank you, but I don't know about doing so well. I'm unemployed and broke, and I was ditched by the man who was both my business partner and my fiancé."

"Remember, you aren't unemployed anymore," he said. "And I'm glad you were ditched."

She grinned at him.

He grinned back, then turned serious. "You weren't the villain in any of that. Reynolds is the bad guy. He conned you."

"He did, but it says volumes about my gullibility."

"Not really," Quint said. "We've got to put our trust in people. There might be a healthy skepticism in that trust, but we still have to believe in others. It's not your fault the man you trusted wasn't trustworthy."

Merlyn felt a lump in her throat and remained silent.

"I don't mean to pry, but what happened with Reynolds?"

"Four years ago, I was working in media relations for a small delivery company and creating websites for my friends on the side," she explained. "I decided to turn my hobby of designing websites into my own company, so I went to a seminar on small businesses."

"Is that where you saw Reynolds?" Quint asked.

Merlyn nodded. "I was impressed that he even remembered who I was. We ended up sitting together and talking during lunch and on breaks. I couldn't believe he wanted to be seen with me. If Reynolds Coltrain thought me worthy, then I was." She clasped her hands in her lap. "And doesn't that make me sound pathetic? Trailer Girl."

"It makes you sound human."

She smiled at him. "You're a nice man."

"Whatever you do, don't tell anyone," he joked. "It'll ruin my tough-guy image."

"My lips are sealed," she said with a grin. "So I told Reynolds what I hoped to do, and he listened. I realize now that while the interest was genuine, it wasn't because he liked me or wanted to encourage me. He was figuring out how to use me."

"Don't be too hard on yourself," Quint said. "Reynolds has been using people his whole life. It's his one talent. He gets away with it because he can be very charming."

Merlyn knew that all too well. "About a week after that initial meeting, he called and asked me out to dinner at the country club." She glanced at Quint. "It probably seems stupid to you because you've gone to the club all your life, but you have no idea what a rush that was for me. From that moment on, I was predisposed to think anything Reynolds said was gold because he liked me enough to take me to the club. Silly me."

"I think it's a badge of honor that you didn't see his deviousness. Why would you? You're not devious and therefore don't automatically see it in others."

Ashley had told her the same thing in a tone that Merlyn had interpreted as complimentary. What was it with these people and thinking gullibility was a good thing? But she couldn't say that out loud, so she simply replied, "Thank you."

"So what happened next?"

"We went into partnership and founded R&M Design. He ran the business end, and I did all the creative work. In many ways, it was a good split. I'd rather design than handle business. Reynolds is not artistic, but he had contacts. We both controlled our own areas of expertise. But that was where I was naive."

"Or maybe he was cunning," Quint suggested. "He saw a smart

but innocent little lamb and set about fleecing her."

Merlyn looked out the window into the darkness. "You'd think growing up with a mother I couldn't trust would make me skeptical and worldly. Not so. At first I read all the contracts, all the letters, everything. But then I got really busy, and Reynolds told me not to worry about the business side. We were getting clients faster than I could produce, and I just signed whatever Reynolds put in front of me."

"I'm not surprised you got so many clients," he said. "Like Dad told you at dinner, we've checked several of the sites you designed. Reynolds was lucky to have you."

She felt a warm glow at his compliment. "And when he asked me to marry him, I thought I had found everything I'd been missing. I had a successful business that was bringing in good money. I was going to get married to my business partner. Finally, my life was stable."

"Did you love him?" Quint asked the question casually, but she knew the answer mattered to him because he wouldn't glance her way.

How could Merlyn tell Quint that she felt more for him in the little time they'd spent together than she'd ever felt for Reynolds? "I thought so."

"You've changed your mind?" He seemed to hold his breath as he waited for her answer.

"Yes, I'm learning there's more to love than security and wish fulfillment," Merlyn admitted. "I equated fulfilling my lifelong dreams with falling in love. I had a business. I was doing work I enjoyed. And I had a guy who paid me lots of attention. No one had ever done that before." She brought her hands to her hot cheeks. "Boy, it's humiliating to admit being that needy."

Quint didn't say anything for a moment, and Merlyn's heart hammered with fear. Had she ruined everything by being so transparent?

He held out his hand toward her, palm up. Then he took his eyes off the road long enough to smile at her.

Merlyn knew she had to take the risk. She reached out and placed her hand in his.

Quint closed his fingers around hers. "I think you are an amazing woman, Merlyn Marshall," he said, his voice husky. "You're tough and beautiful and resilient. I admire you immensely."

Her chest felt so full of relief and joy that she could hardly breathe. "Thank you," she managed to whisper.

They rode in silence for a few minutes, the atmosphere alive and intimate.

Quint pulled into the parking area at the inn, stopped the car, and turned to her. "Before we go in, tell me the rest of the Reynolds story."

Merlyn took a deep breath. "I went to our office one morning, and my keys didn't work. He'd had the locks changed overnight. While I was staring at the door in disbelief, a man was dropped off in the parking lot and climbed into my car. I asked him what he was doing."

In actuality she'd screamed. She'd run to the car and flung the door open. "This is my car. Get out!"

"I've got a work order to bring this car to the garage for a complete overhaul," the man had told her. He held up a piece of paper.

"But it's my car. I never ordered any work on it."

"I don't know about that." The man scanned the paper. "It says here that the owner is R&S Design."

"R&M Design, and I'm the *M*." Merlyn pointed at the logo on the window of the office. She blinked. The gold letters read *R&S Design*. She felt dizzy. Where was the *M*? Who was *S*?

She'd barely heard the man drive away in her car.

"But it wasn't my car," Merlyn now told Quint. "It was the company's car. I tried to call Reynolds and ask what was going on, but every call went straight to his voice mail. And then my phone didn't work at all. My line had been disconnected. Company phone, you see."

"What about your clients?" he asked. "Didn't you contact any of them?"

"Another case of my foolishness. One of the papers I'd signed was a binding agreement saying I couldn't legally contact anyone I'd worked with for five years."

"Reynolds was a thorough scoundrel, wasn't he?"

"Do you think he's clever enough to have planned this whole thing from the beginning?" she asked. "From that lunch at the business seminar?"

"Maybe," Quint replied. "But I think it's more likely that the plan developed as time went on."

Merlyn nodded. "I think you're right. And then Sue Ann came on the scene, and things went into overdrive."

19

Grace

Grace loved singing in the church choir. All these people with adequate voices could blend together to make something truly lovely. She also liked the idea of giving up one's self for the good of many, a lesson that was reinforced every time the choir practiced or sang.

She'd fallen in love with choral singing when a new young music teacher came to her elementary school. While everyone else, especially the boys with their changing voices, loudly bemoaned having to sing, she couldn't wait for their weekly music class. She knew she'd never be asked to sing a solo, but she could sing her heart out in the choir.

Charlotte was a different story. She was a frequent soloist, and her beautiful singing voice could rival the birds who serenaded the coming of each golden dawn.

Shortly before rehearsal began, Grace took her seat, her choir book in hand. She turned to Rochelle, who sat beside her. "How are the plans coming along for this weekend's wedding?"

Rochelle's ready smile lit her face. "Everything's going fine." Then her expression turned thoughtful. "I think."

Grace was caught by the last two words. "Is there something wrong?"

"Not on my end of things," Rochelle said. "It's just a feeling, you know?"

Grace nodded.

"I've done a lot of weddings over the years," Rochelle said. "I can tell if a couple will have a good marriage or if they'll be lucky to last a year. And then there are the women who care only about the wedding, not the marriage."

"Do you think there's something wrong with Paige and Drake?" Grace asked.

Rochelle frowned. "Drake's a nice guy, and Paige is sweet."

"No conflicts between the couple?"

Rochelle shook her head. "I can't put my finger on what's bothering me. The few times I've seen Drake and Paige together, they've been pleasant, cooperative, and polite."

"I thought it was good for young people to have manners," Grace teased.

"Oh, they're not just polite with me. They're polite with each other. Brides and grooms aren't meant to be merely polite."

Grace remembered back to her own wedding. What she'd felt for Hank Porter had not been anything nearly as bland as politeness. Not by a long shot. And when he'd been killed in a horrible accident, part of her heart had died with him. "We'll just have to hope they know what they're doing."

Mimi Beale, the choir director, clapped. "We'll begin in five minutes, people. Finish your conversations."

Rochelle's phone sounded. She checked the screen. "I'd better answer this." She stood and walked out into the hall for privacy.

Charlotte approached Grace, concern etched into her face.

"What's wrong?" Grace asked, startled.

"I've been talking to some of the business owners in town." Charlotte waved a hand to indicate three choir members who were watching her and Grace. "They say the rumor about the caterer is—"

"Oh no! You're sure?" Rochelle's cry echoed from the hall. "We'll talk later."

Everyone stopped what they were doing and turned in her direction.

Rochelle hurried back to the choir loft and stared at Grace and Charlotte. "It's definitely no longer a rumor. The caterer is officially out of business." She sighed. "And the wedding is the day after tomorrow."

Merlyn

Quint pulled Merlyn down beside him on a wicker love seat on the inn's veranda, making her heart sputter with happiness.

The rest of the wedding party as well as Sonja and James joined them.

Merlyn tried to avoid eye contact with Reynolds, Sue Ann, and Hailey. It was all she could do not to squirm under the intensity of their glares.

When everyone was settled in their seats, Quint stood. "Okay, everyone, if you wait here for a minute, I'll be your entertainment for the evening." He turned to Merlyn and said softly, "Save my seat."

Merlyn put her hand on the cushion beside her. "Done." *And with great pleasure.*

Quint left the veranda, disappearing with a plastic garment bag over his arm.

Paige watched her brother's exit with a worried expression. "That's his suit for the wedding, isn't it? I can see the gray of the morning suit through the plastic."

Colton grinned at her. "Just sit back and enjoy."

"*Enjoy* might be too strong a word," Drake said.

Colton turned to Paige. "You know Quint would never do anything to hurt you or ruin your wedding."

Paige nodded, but she seemed even more concerned.

"Why did you choose morning suits?" Merlyn asked to keep Paige from worrying about whatever her brother was about to do.

It worked. Paige's eyes lit up, and she appeared excited, really excited, for the first time all week. "I've seen pictures of the English princes in morning suits, and I think they're so elegant. Even though we're not royalty, we can look just as good."

Merlyn had seen pictures of the princes too. "Tails and top hats?" *Wouldn't that be a kick?*

Drake shuddered. "There's no way I would wear tails or a top hat." The other men muttered agreement.

Paige smiled sweetly at her soon-to-be husband, but her eyes skewered him. "You wouldn't dress like that to make me happy?"

Drake met her stare with one of his own. "You mean you'd ask me to dress like that and make me unhappy?"

The atmosphere suddenly became frosty.

Merlyn sighed. Tails and top hats? That was the molehill they would turn into a mountain?

Before anyone could respond, Quint reappeared in gray trousers and a vest in robin's-egg blue, his jacket dangling from one hand.

Paige leaped to her feet. "No!"

Merlyn bit back a laugh. The trousers on Quint's suit reached his shins.

"You're teasing me," Paige accused. "Stop holding them up. Let them sit naturally at your waist."

"I can't do that in mixed company." Quint held out the waist, and it was several sizes too large. "They'll fall down."

"Oh, how awful!" Hailey rushed over and hugged Paige. "You poor thing."

"Don't cry." Sue Ann patted Paige, even though the bride-to-be showed no signs of crying.

For some reason, Merlyn felt obligated to smooth things over.

"We'll call first thing in the morning and order another suit."

"We?" Sue Ann snapped. "*We'll* call? Who are you to take over? I'm the maid of honor. *I'll* call."

Paige tore her gaze away from Quint. She ignored Sue Ann and glanced at Merlyn. "Yes, that's what we'll do. They can overnight a new outfit. Thank you."

"You're welcome," Merlyn said. She smiled brilliantly at Sue Ann.

The woman appeared startled, then confused.

Merlyn stifled another smile. There really was something to the idea of loving your enemies. It drove them crazy.

"How does the vest fit?" Merlyn asked Quint. "It seems fine."

He patted his chest. "It fits pretty well."

"One less thing to worry about." Merlyn smiled. "See, Paige? It's not as bad as you thought."

"Now you need to see the jacket," Colton said, making no attempt to hide his grin.

Merlyn glanced at Quint, who widened his eyes, and she knew catastrophe was imminent. He threw the jacket to Colton. "Help me get into it."

Still wearing a huge smile, Colton held the coat as Quint slid his arms into the sleeves one at a time, using his free hand to hold up the pants. When he lowered an arm to his side, the jacket covered his hand except for the tip of his longest finger.

Merlyn thought it was a wonder that the coat didn't slip off his shoulders, given its big-and-tall size.

Paige put her hand over her mouth and moaned gently.

Merlyn was torn. She wanted to laugh because the suit was so ridiculous, but she felt Paige's pain that her lovely wedding was turning into a comedy routine.

"What if they don't have any more available suits?" Paige asked her mother, a note of panic in her voice. "Overnight shipping won't mean a thing if there are no suits to ship."

Drake held up his hands. "Don't jump to negative conclusions. We'll get it fixed." His concern would have seemed more genuine if he didn't grin every time he glanced at Quint.

"Can you promise me you can fix this?" Paige asked.

The ill-fitting suit reminded Merlyn of the ruffled dress hanging in her closet. She caught Ashley's eye and imagined that Ashley was thinking the same thing.

Sonja turned to James. "How about your suit?"

"It's perfect. Fits very well."

Quint walked over to his distraught sister and said gently, "I'm sorry. I didn't mean to upset you." He gave her a one-armed hug and a kiss on the temple. "We got such a kick out of how terrible the suit was that we thought you'd laugh too."

Paige crossed her arms over her chest and remained silent.

"Don't worry," Quint went on. "I called the rental company this afternoon to see if we can get another suit in the right measurements by Saturday. They assured me I should have it tomorrow even if they need to drive to the warehouse in Charleston to pick it up."

Paige uncrossed her arms, seeming somewhat pacified. "But what if there aren't any more suits, especially in your size?"

Quint shrugged. "I can wear my dress whites."

"No!" Paige exclaimed. "You'd make the photos unbalanced."

"Take it easy." Drake patted Paige on the back. "It'll all work out."

"Will it?" Suddenly Paige sounded desperate.

Merlyn knew there was more going on here than a poorly fitting suit. More than top hats and tails. More than unbalanced photos. But what?

Grace walked onto the veranda, Winston at her side. She saw

Quint and pressed her lips together to stifle her laugh. "Oh dear."

Charlotte followed close behind her sister. She grinned when she saw Quint. "'Oh dear' is right."

Quint stood at attention, the pose slightly ruined by needing one hand to hold up his pants. "You know morning suits. Always right for the man of distinction."

Rochelle approached the group, clipboard in hand.

Paige pounced on the wedding planner. "You have to fix it!" She motioned to her brother.

"The suit, not me," Quint clarified. "I'm not broken."

"That's debatable," Colton joked.

"The mistake with the suit is mine." Quint spoke easily as he shrugged off the jacket. His relaxed manner somehow brought the emotional temperature on the veranda down several degrees. He smiled at Paige. "I probably sent the wrong figures."

Merlyn studied Quint as he stood there, relaxed and unperturbed. There was no way he'd sent the wrong numbers. She knew it, and so did everyone else. Still, he'd calmed the troubled waters with only a few gentle words.

Paige seemed to get control of her emotions. She even managed a slight smile. "You do look ridiculous."

"As much as I hate to say it," Rochelle broke in, "I'm afraid we have an even more serious problem."

21

Paige

"No! No more problems!" Even as she said it, Paige knew she was being ridiculous. Whether she wanted them or not, problems would come. She was all too familiar with that fact.

Drake put an arm around her shoulders. "It'll be fine. Whatever it is, we'll take care of it. We'll face it together."

Paige resisted the urge to fling Drake's arm off. What was she going to do? If she couldn't stand his arm around her shoulders in company, how was she going to handle the marriage?

Paige glanced around the veranda at her friends and attendants. This group of women was a sorry lot of emotional wrecks, herself included.

Something was upsetting Ashley. She would often get a pained expression and stare off into space. Paige suspected a man was the cause of her unhappiness, even though Ashley never mentioned one.

For all her high-handed ways, Hailey was hurting too. She was losing Quint to someone she didn't like. Unrequited love always hurt. How many years had Hailey pined for Quint? Paige couldn't remember when she hadn't dreamed of marrying him. But it wasn't going to happen.

Merlyn had always had a difficult life with her mother being what she was. The Reynolds and R&M Design disasters were only adding insult to injury. She had started to rise above her beginnings and boom! It had all blown up in her face. But now Quint was interested in her. As Paige thought about it, she realized she felt better about Quint with Merlyn than with Hailey. Merlyn would be kind to him, the way she was to everyone.

And then there were her own problems. Whatever Rochelle had to say couldn't come even close to the severity of her real issues. *No!* She pulled back. She wasn't going there—not tonight, not ever.

Was Sue Ann, cuddled up against Reynolds, the only happy one here? Now there was a disconcerting thought.

These thoughts flew through her mind in seconds. Paige became aware that everyone was watching her, waiting for her reaction to Rochelle's announcement that there was an even more serious problem. She faced Rochelle. "Tell me. I can take it."

"Your caterer has gone out of business as of today," Rochelle announced. "I'm so sorry."

Paige's legs gave out, and she dropped into her chair. The suit fiasco was almost funny and appeared solvable. But no caterer? How could you solve that problem? "How can such a thing happen?"

"They went bankrupt," Rochelle answered. "The bank foreclosed on them and kicked them out of their building."

Paige slapped her hand over her mouth to keep the scream in. Weren't weddings supposed to be special, full of memories that lasted a lifetime? Not for her. She had warring bridesmaids with their own private dramas, ill-fitting clothes, and now no caterer. Enough was enough.

"Oh no!" Sue Ann wailed. "No caterer."

"I can't believe it." Hailey appeared genuinely distressed, except for a little glitter in her eyes. She probably couldn't wait to tell the story of this cursed wedding at the next party she attended.

Paige glanced at Sue Ann, who was clinging to Reynolds, then flicked her gaze back to Hailey. Her two best friends. Paige almost gasped as realization struck her. Sue Ann and Hailey had managed her. For years they'd arranged her life, often at the expense of other people's feelings or wishes, and she'd never minded because they cleared the way for her.

The latest was the chair gambit at afternoon tea when they'd forced Merlyn to sit at a different table. Sue Ann and Hailey thought Paige hadn't seen, but she had. It was like they were thirteen again. She should have said something, done something, but she hadn't. It was easier to let them embarrass Merlyn than step up and say, "What do you think you're doing?"

Heat rose up her neck and face at the acceptance of her own weakness.

"Did you prepay the caterer?" Quint asked Dad.

Paige returned to the present with a painful jolt. She hadn't even thought about the financial ramifications for her parents, only of her own inconvenience. But then this whole wedding was an act of selfishness.

"I paid half," her father answered, sounding resigned. "The rest was due after the ceremony. I guess I'll have to get in line with the rest of their creditors if I want a refund. Maybe I'll end up with pennies on the dollar when all the financials are figured out."

"The bank has literally locked them out." Rochelle shook her head in disbelief. "There are padlocks on the doors."

"Padlocks on the doors?" Sue Ann repeated. "How could the bank do that to them? That is so harsh."

There was a moment of charged silence while everyone seemed to stop breathing.

Merlyn faced Sue Ann. "You've got to wonder how someone could get locked out of their own business, don't you?" she asked, her tone pure saccharine sweetness. "The gall of that bank."

Sue Ann stared at her blankly for a minute. Then comprehension hit her. She turned scarlet and leaned heavily into Reynolds.

"At least the caterer should have had a warning what with the notices the bank must have sent," Merlyn continued. "Sometimes people don't even get that courtesy."

Sue Ann refused to meet anyone's eyes while Reynolds glanced from person to person, silently daring them to say something.

Paige regarded Merlyn with admiration. The sweet kitten had claws after all.

Quint, still holding his pants up, went to stand beside Merlyn in a silent show of support. She smiled at him.

Yes, Paige definitely preferred Merlyn for Quint.

"You're sure there's no way we can at least get the food?" Dad asked.

"I'm not sure there's any food to get," Rochelle admitted. "It sounds like no one would supply them anymore. They're up to their necks in debt with no idea how to get out. It's a shame because they made great food, but they overreached and . . ." She shrugged. "I'm so sorry."

Her mother sighed. "It's not your fault."

"I recommended them," Rochelle said. "When I heard about potential trouble earlier in the week, I called and spoke with the owner. I was assured things were fine and everything was in order for the weekend."

"The guy lied to you," Drake said.

"No, I think it was more wishful thinking," Rochelle responded. "He's poured everything into this business, and it has to break his heart that it's failed. Then I got a phone call this evening at choir practice. It was the caterer himself, confirming everything."

Drake blinked at Rochelle. "What does this mean for the wedding?"

"It means no food," Mom said. "A reception, a beautiful venue, and no food for the guests."

Paige rubbed her forehead. Was this another sign? But how could she possibly back out of the wedding now?

"Wait a second." Merlyn rushed from the veranda into the house. When she returned, she held two books aloft like trophies. She handed one to Mom and gave the other to Paige.

As Paige read the title, she frowned. It was a cookbook. "You want me to cook for my own reception? I can't even boil water without burning it."

Merlyn gestured to the cover of the book. It featured a photo of an elegant dining room. The table was set with sparkling silver and gorgeous china, and the food practically made Paige salivate just by looking at it.

"That dining room seems familiar," Paige said.

Merlyn pointed to the name on the cover. *Charlotte Wylde.*

Paige perked up and turned to Charlotte. "You?" She immediately regretted her foolish question. Of course it was. And the picture was of the inn's dining room.

Mom leafed through the book she held, then gazed at Charlotte with hope in her eyes. "Can you help us?"

Charlotte nodded. "I was about to offer, but Merlyn beat me to it. I would be honored to cater the wedding. Grace and Rochelle and I actually talked about it before we left choir practice. And I've called my friend Dean, who is a fine chef. He's agreed to help too. I can't promise you your original menu because I don't know what we'll be able to get at this late date, but I can promise you good food and plenty of it."

"Dean from The Tidewater?" Paige asked. Dinner there Tuesday night had been wonderful.

"One and the same," Charlotte replied.

Mom hugged her. "We leave ourselves in your capable hands."

They had an answer to the food dilemma—not merely a we'll-get-by answer but a great answer. Paige knew she should feel relieved. She should be happy.

Instead, she swallowed her dread and kept on pretending.

22

Merlyn

Merlyn knew Quint was standing behind her on the veranda before he even spoke. It felt like her heart beat triple time. She had it bad, and it worried her. If someone like Reynolds threw her away, why should she expect someone as extraordinary as Quint to pick up the shattered pieces?

"One catastrophe averted," Quint announced. "We'll get to eat at the wedding."

Merlyn turned. He was still wearing those ridiculous pants and the vest. She pressed her lips together to keep from laughing all over again.

"Go ahead," Quint said. "I can take it."

That was one of the many things she liked about him. He could laugh at himself and didn't mind if others laughed with him.

"Do you think you'll be able to get pants and a jacket that fit?" Merlyn asked.

"I believe so," he said. "When I get the call that the new suit's here, will you go with me to pick it up?"

The idea of time alone with him excited her so much that she became contrary in self-protection. "You can't make the exchange by yourself?"

"I don't *want* to make the exchange by myself," Quint replied. "It's a totally different thing."

Merlyn smiled. "I'd be glad to go with you, assuming Paige doesn't have us doing something on the schedule."

"Don't worry," he said. "I'll get you excused."

"Just not tomorrow from noon on."

"Why? The guys don't have anything special on our schedules tomorrow."

"Well, we're going to the spa for the works."

Quint raised his eyebrows. "I hesitate to ask, but what are the works?"

"A seaweed wrap, a facial, a deep-tissue massage, a manicure, and a pedicure. We'll be absolutely ravishing at rehearsal tomorrow night."

He studied her for a moment. Then he said with a twinkle in his eye that let her know he was both serious and teasing, "How can they improve on perfection?"

Merlyn felt her face flush. "What will you guys do all day?" she asked, changing the subject.

He shrugged. "We'll just hang around The Tidewater and make our own fun."

She could picture the five of them down at the dock doing cannonballs into the water. But no, Reynolds wouldn't do anything so frivolous. "You'll go play golf."

"Maybe," Quint said, grinning.

"Or fish."

"I like to fish."

"Or cruise around the lake rescuing damsels in distress," Merlyn teased.

He took a step closer. "I already rescued the distressed damsel I'm interested in."

She swallowed hard. "You have to stop that."

"Stop what?"

"The over-the-top compliments. Not that I don't appreciate them, but you don't even know me. Not really."

"Which is why I want you to go into town with me," Quint said. "I've enjoyed spending time with you, and I want to get to know you better."

Merlyn wanted to get to know him better too, so badly it scared her. "What about Hailey?" If there was any history there, she needed to be aware.

"I've never given her any encouragement," Quint responded. "In fact, when I'm home, I do my best to stay away from her."

"She's in love with you."

He seemed uncomfortable. "She thinks she is."

Before Merlyn could say anything else, Grace approached them and gestured to a table laden with goodies. "Help yourselves to homemade ice cream with sundae makings."

Quint grinned. "Chocolate sprinkles. I'm in."

"And sugar cones," Merlyn added.

To Merlyn, sugar cones were a symbol of the times her mother had given her enough change to go to the mom-and-pop ice-cream shop in town. The brain freeze from the ice cream and the sweetness of the crispy cone made the long walk to get the treat worth it. She would sit on the bench outside the shop and savor every wonderful bite until she reached the tip of the cone. Then she'd slurp up the sour ball at the bottom of the cone that stopped the ice cream from leaking out. If she had enough self-control, she could make the treat last until she reached home.

She followed Quint over to the table and watched in amazement as he built his sundae. First came a huge helping of chocolate ice cream. Then came sprinkles, bits of candy bars, butterscotch syrup, and finally a mountain of whipped cream topped with mini chocolate chips.

Merlyn was more disciplined with a cone of peach ice cream. Sadly, there were no sour balls to drop in the bottom.

"Come on," he said. "Let's eat down on the dock and watch the moon on the water."

After grabbing a fistful of paper napkins to catch the inevitable drips, Merlyn walked with him across the lawn. They slid into a pair of Adirondack chairs.

The moon blazed a trail across the water, which reached right to Merlyn's feet. "It's so beautiful, and it feels like the moon's all mine."

"It's the angle of incidence being equal to the angle of reflection," Quint said.

Merlyn laughed. "Do you always talk science to the girls you sit with?"

He grinned at her. "It's a winner every time. Melts hearts right and left." Then his expression clouded, and he glanced around to see if anyone was near.

Merlyn took a bite of her cone. "What's bothering you?"

"I'm wondering what's wrong with Paige."

Merlyn caught a drip of ice cream with her napkin before it ran over her hand. She hesitated, wanting to hear what he thought before she gave her opinion. "What do you mean?"

"I'm not sure," he said, sounding confused. "In the past when Paige had boyfriends, she'd be all smiles. She'd talk about the guy constantly until we were sick of hearing his name. I don't expect the grown-up Paige to gush like the junior high or high school Paige, but half the time I think she forgets Drake's about to become her husband. It's more like he's her brother. It worries me."

She nodded. "It's like he's a convenience or a means to an end, not a much-loved future partner."

"So I'm right," Quint said. "I thought it was just me. I'm a guy, and I've lived and worked with guys for the past ten years, so my radar for stuff like that isn't the best." He paused for a spoonful of ice cream. "You said he was a means to an end. What end?"

Merlyn shrugged. "To be a bride? To get married?"

They sat in silence for a few minutes, eating and thinking.

"I even asked her if she was hurrying to get married because she was pregnant." It was Quint's turn to shrug. "I think I offended her."

"What did she say?"

"She said no." He scraped some ice cream from his bowl and took a bite. "I feel like she's setting herself up for a miserable marriage with divorce an inevitable outcome. It's not that Drake isn't a nice guy. He is—for someone kind and low-key. But not for Paige. She'll be bored with him before the honeymoon's over."

"If she's not bored with him already," Merlyn commented.

"Paige is smart. That's what bothers me. She's too smart to make such a big mistake." Suddenly Quint jumped. "What in the world?"

Merlyn grinned as she noticed Locky, practically invisible in the night, sitting in Quint's lap and gazing adoringly at his bowl of ice cream.

Winston joined them. The dog took one glance at Locky and the bowl and recognized a lost cause. He leaped onto Merlyn's lap, where he settled himself with a contented sigh.

Locky ignored everything until Quint had finished his ice cream and disposed of the bowl so the dogs couldn't get at the chocolate remnants inside it. Then he licked Quint's hand and tried to climb into Merlyn's lap with Winston.

Winston held his place, and Locky was forced to settle for a good ear rub. He sighed with pleasure.

Merlyn glanced at the man sitting in the chair next to her.

Quint was watching her with a bemused expression. "They say that dogs are good judges of character."

Another compliment. They were a balm to her spirit after all the criticism she'd received from Reynolds, but she cautioned herself not to get too used to them.

"Do you have any pets?" he asked.

"I had a little fox terrier named Trixie when I was a kid. I was about nine when I found her on the side of the road. She was a puppy, abandoned by someone. She was white with brown spots, and she loved to jump. My mother actually tolerated her and said her name should have been Rabbit. Trixie died shortly after my high school graduation."

"I'm so sorry," Quint said.

"Thanks. I still miss her." Merlyn gazed out over the lake as memories crowded in. "I've always thought God sent her to me because He knew how lonely I was. Sometimes I think Trixie's uncomplicated and unwavering love saved my life."

"It was that bad?"

"Some days it was." She forced a smile. "But I'm here now at this beautiful place." *And with you*, she thought but didn't dare say.

"You're an incredible woman."

Merlyn smiled, glad he couldn't see her scarlet face in the darkness, and changed the subject. "Do you miss the Navy and your life there?"

Quint took his time answering. "Yes and no. I miss the men on my team. I miss the trust and absolute certainty I could depend on them. I even miss the adrenaline rush of danger, but I don't miss the danger itself."

"What made you leave?"

"I could feel my body signaling that I couldn't perform at the high level required much longer. I needed to step aside before someone was hurt because of my diminishing skills."

"You gave up doing something you loved for the sake of others," she concluded. "That's so noble—something a hero would do."

He laughed. "Please don't tell my team that. They'd never let me live it down."

Even though Quint downplayed his motives, Merlyn still thought them—and him—amazing. "So you're going from saving the world through force to saving the developing world with one well at a time. I'm sure you've thought about this, but will your new life be too tame?"

"Yes, I have thought about how I'll adjust," he replied. "I'm an adventure junkie. I admit it. I was driving myself nuts wondering where I could find not just excitement but satisfaction outside the SEALs. Then Dad approached me about joining Water for the World."

"What made you decide to take the job?" she asked.

"I can be a hands-on leader with work like this," Quint said. "I can go to the hard places in the world, not into danger but into creation. I can still save lives, but I don't have to risk my life trying. I can stay around long enough to see a project through. I can see the water flow, the crops get planted, the babies survive."

Merlyn couldn't help but notice the excitement in his voice at the prospect of helping those in need. "Now all I have to do is convey that enthusiasm and commitment to your website."

He leaned forward in his chair. "Yeah, you do. There's so much we need to figure out. How do we keep the wells flowing and the springhouses functioning after we leave? Far too many fall into disrepair when no one knows how to fix them."

Merlyn patted the dogs as she listened to Quint. It was clear that he had been seriously contemplating the many issues the organization faced.

"What kind of a structure do we need to develop to train the nationals to handle the mechanics of these projects?" he continued. "Can we start micro businesses as part of our mission? What are the best possibilities for successful businesses in a given area? What about the parts of the world caught in civil wars? Would we as aid workers be safe? There are so many questions to answer. And many more I haven't even thought of yet."

They were quiet again for a moment. Then Quint said, "And one of these days you'll have to go with us and help with a well."

"Me?" Merlyn asked, sitting up straight.

"Sure. Why not? We'll get you dirty like you've never been dirty

Ashley

Ashley stared at the table filled with ice cream and sundae makings and felt her stomach flip over. She had to get away. She had to.

She watched the milling crowd gathering around the ice cream table and knew she wouldn't be able to sneak into the house. She'd be too visible and would arouse too much concern.

However, the darkness right outside the bright lights of the veranda would require only a few steps, and the night would swallow her. She took one step, then two. After a couple more, she slipped into the welcoming gloom.

Ashley wandered around to the side of the inn, where there was a cozy sitting area by a large magnolia tree. No one would search for her there. She took a seat in the old-fashioned lawn glider and gently pushed the footboards to set it rocking.

In the distance, a gold wash from the lights of downtown Magnolia Harbor lit the night. Here in the yard away from the inn's lights, all was silent and private. She leaned her head back and gazed up at the stars. So beautiful. So mysterious. So far away and beyond mankind's reach.

Ashley snorted. She'd just described her experience with true love—beautiful, mysterious, far away, and beyond her reach.

Thank goodness she didn't live in Reynolds anymore. She didn't think she could bear the possibility of bumping into Drake and Paige, the cheerful newlyweds, every time she went to the grocery store or the gym. She'd stay in Charlotte at least until her heart healed. Then maybe she could come home for visits. But wouldn't coming to Reynolds be like ripping the scab off a wound, resurrecting the pain and forcing the healing back to day one? She sighed. Maybe she could never go home again.

But if she didn't go home, her parents would camp out on her doorstep until she went back to her monthly visits. Her sister would stare her down until Ashley confessed her pain about Drake, and then she would find Drake and give him a piece of her mind. Her brother would look Drake up and "accidentally" break his nose. And she didn't even want to think about what her aunts and uncles and cousins would do.

Of course, Ashley was exaggerating her family's reactions, but it was wonderful to be so loved. Maybe it was because she grew up watching her father love her mother, but it was agony *not* to be loved by the one who mattered most.

A noise drew her attention, and she saw Drake walking across the lawn toward her. He was the last person she wanted to see while she wallowed in self-pity. "Go away."

His step hitched a bit, but he kept coming.

"Go away," Ashley repeated. "People will see."

"I don't care. Do you?" Drake took the other side of the glider, putting them knee to knee. "We need to talk."

"No, we don't. There's nothing more to say. Please allow me to feel the fool in private."

"You are not a fool."

"I must be since I saw something that wasn't there."

He leaned toward her, intent and determined. "There was something there. At least for me there was."

Ashley pulled back, staring at him in disbelief. He'd felt something? Was he serious? "Don't you dare say that."

"But I do care for you," Drake admitted. "I don't like to see you so sad."

She scowled at him. "You're not allowed to care for me. You're not allowed to be concerned because I'm sad. You're marrying someone else."

"You don't need to remind me." He leaned his head back, studying the stars. "I know."

Ashley wanted to stay mad at him, but a little seed of sympathy nudged her heart. He was so clueless. "Paige is a wonderful woman. You should be happy."

"I can't stop thinking about what you said this afternoon." Drake grabbed her hand.

She knew she should pull free, but she couldn't. "What did I say?"

"You said if you got what you wanted, it would be good. You said it would be wonderful." He took a big breath. "You're right."

Why was he telling her this? Talk about ripping the scab off a wound. "And you think you know what I want?"

Drake faced her. "I do. Because it's what I want too."

For a moment, Ashley couldn't breathe. "It's what you want too? Then why did you propose to Paige if you had even a shred of affection for me?"

He played with their joined hands, threading their fingers together. "I keep going back over everything, trying to figure it out. Paige asked me to take her to the country club for the spring dance because she didn't want to go alone. She's a good friend, and our other friends were going together as a group, so why not? It wasn't a date."

"But it was, at least to her and everyone else."

Drake nodded. "Suddenly Paige was everywhere I was, talking to me, sitting with me. Then she told me she'd be glad to be my wife. I honestly don't remember ever asking her to marry me. She wanted to use her grandmother's diamond, so I never even bought a ring. Before I could blink, I was engaged and everyone was thrilled for us."

"And you were finally going to be a Reppert."

"What? No!" He sounded appalled at the thought.

"Oh yes," Ashley insisted. It was as if the sun of understanding broke through the dark clouds of confusion. Drake could deny it if he wanted, but Ashley knew she had hit on the one thing he had always yearned for—a family who loved him. If he married Paige, he would get that dream at last.

The truly sad thing was that her family would have given him that same love and acceptance. But she couldn't tell him because then he might want her for the same unacceptable reason that he found himself about to marry Paige. She would settle for no less than his loving her with all his heart.

Ashley jerked her hand free. "Go away and leave me alone," she said, forcing the words through a throat clogged with tears.

When she looked up, he was gone. Somehow that wasn't any better.

Grace

Friday morning after breakfast had been served, Grace peered into the kitchen, Winston at her heels. Charlotte and Dean Bradley from The Tidewater were busy preparing for the wedding reception.

Charlotte was on the phone placing an order. "You've got it? Wonderful." She consulted the piece of paper in her hand. "Now I also need . . ."

Grace almost felt sorry for the supplier as Charlotte continued to read from her list.

Dean scribbled on a piece of paper, revising his own list as he heard what Charlotte was ordering. "Vidalias. Don't take any other kind. And double that order of heirloom tomatoes."

"You'll get your turn." Charlotte waved him away and continued talking to the supplier. "You get it all together, and my sister will be there within the hour to pick it up."

So Grace was to be courier. She didn't mind. It was a nice day for a drive.

"Now Dean wants to talk to you," Charlotte said, then handed off the phone.

Dean greeted the supplier and began reciting from his list.

Grace walked over to her sister. "Let me get my purse while Dean finishes with his order. Then I can go."

Charlotte opened the dishwasher, and clouds of steam filled the air. She began to unload the clean breakfast dishes as if the plates weren't hot enough to toast marshmallows on. "Take your CR-V. You'll need the space."

As if Grace had another car. She glanced down at Winston. "Want to go for a ride?"

The little dog yipped and danced in excited circles.

Smiling, Grace started for her private quarters to freshen her lipstick and grab her purse and car keys.

When the bell above the front door chimed, Winston left Grace's side and detoured to the lobby.

Grace followed. She grinned as Winston bounded over to Winnie, who had just stepped inside. Her aunt carried a small booklet that sported a pretty, multicolored floral cover.

"Do they have you working in the kitchen too?" Grace asked, giving Winnie a hug.

"No. Why do you ask?"

"The caterer went out of business, and Charlotte's doing the wedding tomorrow with Dean's help," Grace explained. "But don't tell him that. He thinks he's doing the wedding with Charlotte's help."

"Of course," Winnie said. "It's all over town. Gus and I went out for breakfast, and the place was buzzing. Sentiment seems equally divided between sympathy for the poor caterer and admiration for the way Charlotte and Dean stepped up."

Grace shook her head, amazed at the speed of gossip. "Life in Magnolia Harbor certainly holds no mystery or secrets."

"Especially if you want to keep them secret," Winnie added.

The front door opened, and Grace and Winnie turned to see Quint entering, head down and thumbs flying as he texted.

"How do they do that so fast?" Winnie mimed texting with her thumbs. "I have to poke one letter at a time with my index finger."

"It's an age thing."

"Well, they're all going to have arthritic thumbs by the time they're forty," Winnie muttered.

Grace had to laugh. "Good morning, Quint."

He glanced up from whatever he was reading, a smile creasing his handsome face. Grace took that to mean Merlyn would be right down. "Good morning, ladies." Quint's smile was charming. Grace had no trouble understanding why Merlyn was enchanted with the man. "My suit for the wedding arrived this morning."

"That's wonderful news," Grace said.

"We're going to return the suit I have to the rental place." Quint kept glancing up the stairs. "It's a couple of towns over, so I want to leave right away."

"But your suit was so special," Grace teased, grinning at the memory.

He rolled his eyes. "I'm getting one that fits, I hope."

Grace nodded. "I like a positive thinker."

"Yeah, that's me." Quint looked up again as footsteps sounded on the stairs, then turned to Grace with a twinkle in his eyes. "Especially about certain things."

Grace and Winnie exchanged delighted glances, thoroughly taken with the romance unfolding before them.

Charlotte hurried from the kitchen and thrust two pieces of paper into Grace's hand. "Check everything against the lists. Make certain everything is fresh. No wrinkles, blemishes, or spots."

Grace scanned one of the lists. "What's this?" She pointed at some chicken scratch. "And this?"

"Dean never could write so others could read it." Charlotte sighed and snatched the papers out of Grace's hand. "Forget it. I'll go."

"What?" Grace held out her hand. "You can't go. You have things to do."

"But I can't do them until I have these supplies." Charlotte turned back to the kitchen and almost plowed into Dean, who had appeared behind her.

"I'll go," he offered. "I want to check everything myself."

Charlotte bristled at his comment. "You don't trust me to check?"

"That's not what I said," Dean replied, narrowing his eyes at her.

"Well, it's what you meant," Charlotte said.

At this rate, they'd be lucky to have any food at the reception. Grace decided to interrupt before the ancient history between these two became an all-out brawl. "Why don't you both go? That way, you can each check your own orders."

Charlotte nodded, appearing the tiniest bit chagrined.

"Yeah," Dean mumbled.

Charlotte and Dean turned, debating whose car had the most room, and disappeared into the kitchen.

"They do very well when he's cooking across the lake and she's cooking here," Grace remarked.

"They'll be fine." Winnie waved her hand dismissively. "I think they enjoy bickering with each other."

"Their fun is nerve-racking for me," Grace said.

Quint turned to Grace. "On behalf of my sister and my family, I want to thank you and Charlotte for all you're doing to make Paige's day special."

Grace liked this young man. "It's our pleasure. Now you go get your suit so we can all relax about that part of the wedding."

Quint nodded and held out his hand to Merlyn.

Grace watched with delight as a flush turned the young woman's cheeks a lovely rose.

"Wait a minute." Winnie handed Merlyn the booklet she'd been holding. "This is for you."

"For me?" Merlyn ran a hand over the pretty flowers. "What a beautiful cover. It's like an old English garden."

Winnie patted Merlyn's hand. "I know it's only half useful, but I also know you need it."

Merlyn opened the booklet. "It's a calendar." She lifted the ribbon in the middle marking the current week. She glanced up with a confused expression, but she was polite as ever. "Thank you."

Winnie smiled, nodded, and turned to go. "My work here is done."

Grace watched her aunt walk out the door, then turned to Merlyn. "I have no idea why she felt you needed a calendar, but don't lose it. All I can tell you from previous experience is that her gifts are usually right on the nose."

"I can write in Water for the World meetings and deadlines," Merlyn told Quint.

He nodded. "Or dates with me."

Merlyn blushed again.

Grace watched the pair leave and murmured to Winston, "I wonder if they'll come back here for their wedding."

Winston cocked his head as if questioning her.

Grace smiled. "Oh, I just know."

Rochelle rushed in, clipboard in hand. "I was in the barn with the florist, and I got a call. You won't believe the latest mess."

Merlyn

Merlyn sat in the passenger seat of Quint's Jeep Cherokee and flipped through the calendar. "Why did Winnie give this to me? She doesn't even know me."

"The gift of a calendar halfway through the year is a bit unusual," Quint admitted.

"Well, it was a nice gesture." She slid it into her large purse. "So you got a call that your suit's in."

He nodded. "Apparently, someone from the rental company drove all the way to Charleston this morning to get it."

"Paige will be relieved," Merlyn said. "And now you won't have to wear your dress whites."

"I wouldn't want to make the photos unbalanced." Quint grinned. "Which is good since I don't have them with me."

She laughed. "You neglected to mention that detail last night."

"If there's one thing the service has taught me, it's the importance of timing." He glanced over at her. "Tell me something about yourself that I don't know."

Oh my. Merlyn's stomach flipped. She had known that if he was genuinely interested in her, he'd ask questions. He should ask questions. She planned to ask him lots of things too, like his favorite color, favorite teams, worst high school memory. What kind of a brother was he? Who invented the eye-widening thing? Had he always planned to be a SEAL? What did he believe about God?

But right now, he was asking about her, and Merlyn felt embarrassed. What could she say? Should she tell him about the nights she'd gone to bed hungry? Or the time Mom had squandered the money that was supposed to pay the electric bill and the lights went off until her next payday? Or how, when Merlyn was eight years old, she'd started taking money from her mom's purse in order to pay the propane man in the winter so they'd have heat? Even today Merlyn felt guilty about that. It made her a thief. She could tell herself she'd had no choice and know that was true, but sneaking was still sneaking and stealing was still stealing.

"Is it that bad?" Quint asked gently, sympathy in his eyes.

The expression on his face bothered her. "Do me a favor and don't feel sorry for me. I don't handle sympathy well." Especially from someone she wanted to think highly of her.

He seemed surprised for a moment. "Got it. No sympathy. Is it okay if I admit that I admire you?"

"So you've said, but why?" Merlyn asked. "I've never done anything particularly worthy. In fact, I've done many foolish things, as you already know."

"Don't give Reynolds that much power. He's only one little blip in an amazing life."

"He's one big blip in my recent life," she corrected.

Quint shook his head. "One day soon you'll look back and realize his unconscionable behavior opened new and better doors for you."

Merlyn studied him. Was such a thing possible?

"You don't believe me?"

"It seems unlikely at the moment," she said. "Maybe I'll agree sometime way in the future when I don't feel like an idiot every time I think about how gullible I was."

"We've already agreed that trusting him was not a sign of either idiocy or gullibility," he reminded her. "And trusting people is a risk we have to take. So sometimes we get burned. Next time we're smarter."

"You almost make me feel like I should get a gold star for being snookered," she teased.

"You're a woman with great survival skills. I admire anyone who not only survives but thrives despite everything being stacked against them."

Merlyn blinked. She liked being considered a survivor and a thriver, especially after years of feeling inferior because of Reynolds.

Quint flicked on his turn signal and turned onto Main Street. "I haven't met your mom yet."

Merlyn stopped breathing for a moment. He hadn't met her mom *yet*? Did that mean what she thought? Oh, how she hoped it did.

"But I know she's a lot different than mine," he continued.

Merlyn's laugh was without humor. "What an understatement. Your mom is what moms are supposed to be. My mom? Not so much."

"Tell me about her," Quint coaxed.

"I don't want you to think she was all bad," Merlyn said. "Her friends love her. She's somehow managed to keep the same job as a cashier at the grocery store for years. And sometimes she would come through for me."

She told him the story of the infamous birthday party, leaving out the part about never actually getting to the party. "She was so proud of herself for helping me, for being a good mom."

"Where does your strength come from?" he asked.

"My strength?" Merlyn echoed. Too many times, especially since the Reynolds fiasco, she'd felt anything but strong.

"You put yourself through college. You started a business. You create wonderful projects for your clients. And you did it all without financial or emotional help from your family."

She'd had no choice. It was push ahead, or she'd become her mother. It felt as if her heart stopped beating as the truth slammed into her.

That was it, wasn't it? That had been her fear and her motivation all these years. "I'm afraid I'll become my mother."

Quint reached over and grabbed her hand. He held tight. "Never."

Merlyn pressed her free hand over her heart to try to calm it and repeated, "I'm afraid I'll become my mother." How had she never seen it before?

"No, you won't," he said. "You're a strong woman where she's weak. You've made wise choices that have had positive results. She's made poor choices that have caused pain."

Quint was right. Merlyn understood wise choices and positive results. What she hadn't understood until now was the deep fear that prompted everything she did.

"Growing up, I vacillated between anger and pity for my mom," she admitted. "The older I got, the more I leaned toward pity. She became a single mom at sixteen. Her family gave her no help, and her boyfriend disappeared. She was a teenager who couldn't handle her own life, let alone mine. Eventually I understood that she did the best she could."

"Is there any chance that she'll get help?" he asked.

She shook her head. "Not so far. But I keep praying."

Quint lifted her hand to his lips and kissed it. "As I said before, I admire you."

Admiration was nice, but she really, really wanted more. She stayed quiet, hoping he would continue.

"I like you a lot, and I want to keep getting to know you better," he confessed.

Merlyn grinned. "Me too."

Her phone rang, interrupting the moment. She reached into her purse, removed the phone, and answered the call.

Grace's voice came through loud and clear. "We've got trouble."

26

Merlyn

Merlyn's heart sank. What else could go wrong with this wedding?

"Is there a problem?" Quint asked.

She nodded and mouthed, "It's Grace."

"Put it on speaker," he said.

Merlyn nodded and pressed the button.

Grace's urgent-sounding voice filled the car. "Ren Best, the baker, just called Rochelle. He has to leave for a family emergency."

Merlyn gasped. "Now?" *The day before the wedding?* "So we won't have a cake?" That would be disappointing but nowhere close to the catastrophe of a bride and groom who shouldn't marry.

"No, the cake is ready," Grace said. "Ren says he stayed up half the night to finish it."

"What a relief," Merlyn said. "So what's the issue?"

"He has to go in fifteen minutes, or he'll miss his plane," Grace said.

Merlyn wondered why Grace was telling her this. They were a few towns away from Magnolia Harbor, so they wouldn't be able to get to the bakery in time.

"The bakery is in the same town as the rental shop," Grace explained. "I asked if Ren could wait until you got there since you're already in the area for the suit."

Merlyn glanced around. "We're on Main Street at the stoplight by the gas station. What's the address?"

As Grace recited it, Quint punched it into his GPS.

"Go around to the rear of the building," Grace said. "He'll be watching for you. Rochelle is talking to him now, relaying the information about your imminent arrival."

Quint peered at the GPS screen. "It's only two blocks from here."

When the light turned green, he took a side street and drove down the alley behind the row of buildings where the bakery was located. He stopped at the door with the bakery's name stenciled on it, then maneuvered the Jeep so the hatchback was even with the door.

Merlyn climbed out of her side as Quint exited his. They hurried to the hatchback, and Quint lifted it so it would be ready to load.

A tall man with short black hair opened the door and frantically motioned them inside.

Merlyn and Quint followed him into a kitchen filled with huge ovens, long stainless steel counters, and pans, bowls, and utensils hanging everywhere. In the center of one counter sat several tiers of a wedding cake. To Merlyn's relief, the tiers were frosted and ready.

"You'll have to assemble the cake yourselves," Ren told them. "I haven't put it together because I didn't know if it would fit in your car."

Quint studied the four tiers. "My Jeep's tall enough."

"Unfortunately, I don't have time to assemble it now. Our daughter and her husband were in a terrible accident, and my wife and I need to go."

"I'm so sorry," Quint said. "Don't worry about this. Tell us what to do."

"The layers are to be set on these columns." Ren pulled a few columns from a pile of several in a clear plastic bag. "I decided to use the columns because the tiers need to be separated. The top one is specially made because someone's allergic to eggs."

Merlyn sighed. *Reynolds.*

Ren tried to keep a professional face on things, but a crack showed in his manner as he said, "Have you ever made a cake with rice flour and no eggs to bind things together? Because of the allergies, this tier mustn't touch the other layers."

Quint eyed the cake like a time bomb about to detonate. He squared his shoulders. "We'll take care of it."

Ren checked his watch. "I need to hurry. I don't want to miss our plane. Grab a tier."

Merlyn stared, aghast. Grab a tier? Was he kidding? She felt like hiding her hands behind her back. She wasn't going to be the one who ruined Paige's wedding cake.

When Ren picked up a tier, she noticed that each one rested on a sturdy piece of cardboard. Relief flooded through her. All she had to do was hold her piece of cardboard steady, and everything would be fine. She lifted one, being extra careful not to trip over something and drop her tier. She followed Ren and Quint out the door.

Ren carefully put his layer in the car first and oversaw the placement of Merlyn's and Quint's. He hurried back into the kitchen, Merlyn and Quint on his heels.

"Get the top tier," Ren told Quint, pointing to the lone remaining round of cake rimmed with piping and sporting a little square in the middle where the topper would go.

Quint took the top tier as instructed.

Ren picked up a cake stand while Merlyn snagged the plastic bag of columns.

"Don't forget these." Ren grabbed the columns he'd removed from the bag to show them how the cake was to be constructed and tucked them under his arm. "You'll need them to have the correct number."

Quint followed Ren to the vehicle, and Merlyn and her bag of columns brought up the rear.

As soon as Merlyn was out the door, Ren handed her the cake stand, pulled a key from his pocket, and locked the door. "The florist will put real flowers on the cake tomorrow so they'll be fresh. Daisies and rosebuds,

I think. She and I have talked about it. She knows what she's doing."

Merlyn smiled. Daisies and rosebuds, the same flowers that would make up the bridal party's halos and bouquets.

The baker's phone rang.

Ren took the cake stand back from Merlyn and set it into the Jeep with the loose columns. "I've got to take this call," he said, removing his phone from his pocket. "It might be about the kids."

"We've got it from here," Quint assured him. "Thanks for everything."

"It's my wife," Ren reported, then spoke into the phone. "I'm leaving now. I'll be there to pick you up in a few minutes. We'll make it. Don't worry." He disconnected and shoved the phone into his pocket, then took the top tier from Quint and placed it into the vehicle.

"Go," Quint ordered.

"Gone." With a nod, Ren sprinted for his car.

He was only a cloud of dust at the end of the alley when Merlyn realized she was still holding the bag of columns. She climbed into the passenger seat and held the bag on her lap.

Quint got in and glanced over his shoulder at the back compartment. "I want to get rid of this cake as quickly as possible. I couldn't face Paige if I wrecked her wedding cake."

"You still have to get your suit," Merlyn reminded him.

"It'll only take a few minutes," he said as he slowly drove out of the alley and returned to Main Street.

"Or so we hope."

Quint parked in front of the rental shop, then grabbed the ill-fitting suit from where it was hanging. They rushed into the store.

Merlyn and the clerk in the shop both urged him to try on the new suit to make sure it fit.

He walked from the dressing room looking more handsome than any prince, at least to Merlyn.

They returned to the car in less than fifteen minutes. Merlyn slid into the Jeep while Quint peeked into the back.

"Everything's fine," he announced as he climbed into the driver's seat. Relief was evident in his voice.

Merlyn didn't know what he expected to happen to the cake while they'd been gone, but she had to admit she was also anxious to get it safely to its destination.

During the ride to the inn, Quint and Merlyn were mostly silent as they listened to the radio. The trip was a little tense but without incident. Merlyn sighed in relief as they reached the inn's driveway. They'd made it. The wedding cake was safe and sound.

Then Quint turned into the driveway.

Merlyn heard a rolling noise that made her go cold all over. She spun around but couldn't see over the back seat. She rose onto her knees and gasped.

What had once been the beautiful top layer of Paige's cake was now a disaster.

Paige

Paige gaped at her ruined wedding cake in Quint's car. "It makes me think of Humpty-Dumpty. Only much worse."

Quint, Mom, Grace, Rochelle, and all the bridesmaids stood in a semicircle around the open hatchback of Quint's SUV. Charlotte was still on her supplies run with Dean. Grace held Winston, whose nose twitched at the sweet smells emanating from the vehicle. Mom gripped Locky firmly by the collar as he strained toward the treat mere feet away.

"What happened?" Hailey demanded, her voice as sharp as if Quint and Merlyn had destroyed the cake on purpose.

Quint turned slightly green when he glanced at the mess.

Paige thought he should feel bad. First, he gave her a heart attack with his awful suit, and now this. He was becoming a one-man wedding wrecker.

Quint cleared his throat. "The top tier of the cake was accidentally put on a pair of the columns lying flat in the car. When I turned into the driveway, the columns rolled and took the cake with them. When the cake bumped into the side of the car, it crumbled."

"No eggs," Merlyn mumbled.

"How did it get put on the columns?" Hailey asked with all the force of a prosecuting attorney going after a hostile witness. She fixed her glare on Merlyn.

"In his hurry to leave so he wouldn't miss his flight, Ren unintentionally set the cake on the pair of columns he'd pulled from the bag," Merlyn explained, clutching the plastic bag of columns tighter.

Hailey put her hands on her hips. "So you're blaming the man who isn't here to defend himself? How nice."

Paige frowned at Hailey. She was coming to dislike her friend's tart tongue.

"You're right, Hailey." Merlyn held up the bag. "I was in charge of the columns. I should have noticed."

Hailey blinked, nonplussed.

Paige realized that Merlyn might have figured out how to defang Hailey. If someone agreed with her condemnation, she didn't know what to do.

"It wasn't your fault, Merlyn," Quint said. "It was all mine."

Paige studied her brother as he defended the woman he was obviously falling for. She'd never thought he'd show anyone such preferential treatment. Of course, the only times she'd seen him in the last ten years were when he was home on leave, and then he spent all his energy trying to distance himself from Hailey.

"Don't worry," Rochelle said. "We'll fix it."

Paige shook her head. "Not even Charlotte with her magical culinary talents is going to put this collection of crumbs back together."

"No, I mean the flowers and the rest of the cake," Rochelle clarified. "The other three tiers are still perfect."

"And they aren't as fragile," Merlyn said. "They've got eggs."

"What's all this about eggs?" Hailey snapped.

"Reynolds," Paige explained. "One layer doesn't have eggs because of his allergies."

They all regarded the sad remains once more.

"But the flowers will fix it," Rochelle said. "The cake will be gorgeous."

Mom nodded. "And I'm sure it'll be delicious."

Grace stepped forward and picked up one of the undamaged tiers. "Let's get these in the house and out of the heat to keep them fresh for tomorrow."

Rochelle and Ashley took the other two tiers and followed Grace toward the inn.

Merlyn retrieved the columns responsible for the calamity and shook them free of cake pieces. She slid them into her bag of columns.

Paige stared at the crumbled cake and smeared frosting in Quint's Jeep. How were they going to clean up this mess?

"I'll be back in a minute with supplies to help clean up the car," Grace called over her shoulder as if she'd read Paige's mind.

Paige relaxed, glad to let Grace take charge.

"I'll help too," Ashley called.

"And me," Rochelle said.

Sue Ann and Hailey followed the women to the inn. They didn't offer to help as they disappeared from view.

Paige turned her back on the crumbs and leaned against the side of the SUV.

Mom reached for her hand. "Are you okay, sweetheart?"

"I'm fine." Paige's smile was almost sincere. "It's only a cake."

Her mom looked aghast. "It's your wedding cake."

"I know." Paige was proud she wasn't getting hysterical about things, but shouldn't she feel something? A bride should feel terrible if her wedding cake was damaged. Well, this bride didn't, and her lack of distress was in itself distressing.

Mom and Merlyn reached into the car and collected the bigger chunks of cake. They piled them on top of the cardboard. Soon their fingers were covered in icing.

"I'm so sorry, Paige," Quint said for the fifth or sixth time.

Paige waved her hand. "Don't worry about it. It was an accident." Was it God sending her another sign? She rubbed her hands up and down her arms. If it was, she didn't know what to do about it.

Her mother regarded the piece of cake in her hand, then popped it into her mouth.

"Mom!" Paige chided, though why she was upset about her mom eating a piece of the ruined cake she didn't know.

"Not bad," her mother said.

Merlyn studied the piece of cake she'd just picked up. She glanced at Paige as if asking her permission.

"Go for it," Paige said.

Merlyn did. "Pretty good for rice flour and no eggs."

Curious, Paige selected a piece that was mostly icing. The sweetness melted on her tongue. "Great frosting."

Mom turned to Merlyn, her eyes twinkling. "What a shame. It was Reynolds's layer."

Merlyn put her hand to her mouth as if to hide her smile. "Yes, it was."

"Very sad." Quint ran a finger over a clump of icing and stuck it into his mouth. "And it's quite tasty. Poor Reynolds. He'll never know."

"You guys are terrible," Paige admonished, but she couldn't help smiling as she reached for more.

"It couldn't have happened to a more deserving guy," her mom said, then popped another piece into her mouth.

Suddenly the four of them were laughing so hard that tears ran down their faces.

28

Merlyn

Merlyn ran up to her room for a few minutes before she met Quint for lunch. She kept smiling every time she thought of their laughter over the ruined cake tier. She couldn't believe how Reynolds was losing his power to hurt her and all because other people she valued actually liked her.

She was brushing her hair when her phone rang. She stared at it for a moment. Who would be calling her? She'd given her new number to very few people.

Her lifelong fear surfaced as it always did when her personal phone rang. Something terrible had happened to her mother. Her heart began to pound, and she felt cold and clammy all over.

Merlyn glanced at the screen. She didn't recognize the number, but the area code wasn't from home. Relief rippled through her. Whatever it was, it probably wasn't about her mom. She answered.

"Merlyn?" a rich female voice asked. "This is Celia Belasco."

"Celia?" she echoed. The nationally known inspirational speaker and writer whose website she'd been working on when Reynolds had kicked her out? The client whose website would have put R&M irrevocably on the map? She must have misheard.

"I thought you were dead," Celia announced.

"What?" Merlyn gave a little disbelieving laugh. Of all the bad things that had happened to her over the past months, dying was one of the few she hadn't experienced. Maybe she had something to be thankful for in the R&M fiasco after all. She was still alive.

"I've been mourning the loss of the world's greatest Web designer these past three months," Celia went on.

The compliment was a balm to Merlyn's spirit. "What made you think I was dead?"

"Reynolds."

"He told you I was dead?" Merlyn had wondered how he explained her sudden absence to her former clients, but it had never crossed her mind that he would tell people she was deceased.

"When I called to talk with you, he told me you were gone. He paused dramatically before he said 'gone,' and he sounded choked up. I asked if you were dead, and he repeated that you were gone. What else was I to think?"

"I can't believe it." Merlyn flopped onto the white love seat at the foot of her bed and put her feet on the blue velvet ottoman. "How did you get my number?" she asked, then quickly added, "Not that I mind."

"My personal assistant has been scouring every form of social media for anything with your name so we could send a gift in your memory," Celia explained. "She finally noticed something about your being in a wedding."

"Yeah, I'm in a wedding tomorrow, but I didn't post anything about it."

"No, it was someone named Paige."

"Right," Merlyn said. Certainly neither Sue Ann nor Hailey would have mentioned her.

"Anyway," Celia continued, "we knew you weren't dead, so we started calling all the churches in a fifty-mile radius of Reynolds, using my name shamelessly. 'Do you know the wonderful Merlyn Marshall, and if so, would you please give us her phone number?' One of them finally put us in touch with your mother."

Merlyn swallowed. "I'll bet that was an interesting conversation."

"Actually it was. She told us all about Reynolds's locking you out of the office. She was quite angry on your behalf."

"Really?" *And several pigs were sighted flying by on their way to Florida, carrying suitcases in their little hooves.* How like her mother to tell Merlyn she deserved everything that happened to her but to defend her to an outsider.

"With a mother like that, no wonder you're such a sweetheart," Celia remarked.

"Thanks," Merlyn replied. "Well, even though I'm alive and well, I don't think I'm supposed to talk to you."

"Why not?" Celia asked. "After all I went through to find you, you'd better talk to me."

"I'm legally not allowed to talk to you," she clarified.

"Your mother told me to go for it and ignore anything Reynolds did."

"My mom wasn't the one who spoke with a lawyer," Merlyn pointed out. "I inadvertently signed a paper—"

"I don't care what you signed," Celia interrupted. "I need your help."

"And I would love to help you, but I can't," Merlyn said.

"What did the paper you signed say?" Celia demanded. "And how did Reynolds trick you into signing it?"

"How do you know he tricked me?"

"Because he tricked me!" Celia's outrage carried clearly through the ether.

Merlyn had to smile. In a weird way, Celia's anger toward Reynolds was comforting. "When he gave me the papers to sign, he told me not to concern myself with them. He said he'd take care of everything on the business side so I could focus on being creative."

Celia snorted.

"After Reynolds locked me out, he sent me copies of all the relevant papers I'd signed," Merlyn continued. "By special messenger."

"How thoughtful of him," Celia said sarcastically.

Her tone gave Merlyn a boost for a moment before her distress kicked in again. "I took the papers to an attorney, and he told me they're legally binding. One of them says I'm not allowed to contact any former clients for five years."

"But you didn't contact me," Celia argued. "I contacted you. My assistant and I will swear to it in court if it comes to that."

Were they splitting hairs, or was it actually okay since Celia had been the one to contact Merlyn? Was there a possibility they could work together again? Merlyn tried not to get her hopes up.

"You know how we were working on updating my website before you disappeared?" Celia asked. "We were selecting clips from talks I'd given."

Merlyn nodded as if Celia could see her. "Sure. We were in the process of pulling video clips from four or five of your TV and conference talks. We were also choosing crucial quotes from your books."

"Right. I sent you several professional photos and a bunch of candid shots from the last trip to the orphanage in Africa and the one in Mexico to go with the giving information. We were going to redesign my blog and offer a couple of podcasts. And we were setting up a registration page for live streaming of the conference scheduled for October."

"I'm sorry that I didn't get to finish what we started," Merlyn said genuinely. Leaving clients with partially completed projects was one of the most disturbing parts of Reynolds's actions. "Is R&S taking care of you?" She didn't expect them to be. Why else would Celia be calling her? On the other hand, she couldn't imagine Reynolds allowing one of his biggest clients to get lost in the shuffle.

"Let me tell you," Celia said, her tone portending catastrophe.

Merlyn held her breath, hoping for Celia's sake that things weren't too bad.

"Sue Ann, whoever she is, does not know what she's doing. When Reynolds introduced her to me, he said she was on the cutting edge of the latest technology and trends and would exceed you. I didn't know how that was possible, but I decided to give her a chance."

Merlyn had wondered if Sue Ann had the technical know-how to work with the more sophisticated sites like Celia's. As far as she knew, Sue Ann had earned a degree in psychology and worked as a guidance counselor at the consolidated high school before helping to force Merlyn out at R&M. Merlyn had been a Web design major with an art minor, and she'd worked in the field for several years, keeping up with technological advancements that occurred every day.

"Talk about fussy and overblown and confusing and without pattern," Celia ranted. "It's my material, and I can't even find half of it on my own website."

Merlyn pressed her lips together to keep from smiling and chided herself. She would not be pleased that Sue Ann didn't live up to Reynolds's hype because she did not want to be that type of person. She liked justice, not vengeance. But she had to admit she also liked vindication.

"It's terrible," Celia went on. "How are women who come to my site supposed to find any information? Links have disappeared or don't work. Pictures have the wrong captions. And the contact page has an incorrect phone number."

"Oh no. I'm so sorry."

"Me too. Now fix it for me."

Merlyn got up and started pacing, her mind churning with thoughts and ideas. And the one big impediment to going forward. "I don't have the codes to get into the site."

"Then I'll fire Reynolds, and we'll start a new site," Celia responded. "We've got to do something before she damages my reputation and the reputation of my ministry. I cannot afford to appear unprofessional."

"I know it's distressing," Merlyn said. "But keep in mind that Sue Ann and Reynolds don't have the power to undermine your much-respected ministry."

"I realize that it's an overstatement, but the site is my face to the world. You made me look good, but Sue Ann—not so much."

Merlyn's heart was racing. Last night she got Water for the World as a client. Today Celia called, and the woman had a large network of speaker and writer friends she had brought to R&M. "I would love to work with you again, but honestly I have to check with my lawyer to see if I legally can."

"Listen to me," Celia said sternly. "I can ruin Reynolds with a few well-placed phone calls if he gives you any trouble. I don't want to. It's not a nice thing to do, and I think he's doing a very good job of ruining his business all by himself. But I can sink him if that's what it takes to get you back on my team."

Merlyn wasn't proud that vengeance sounded so attractive. At a word from her, Reynolds and Sue Ann could get what they deserved.

"'Vengeance is Mine, I will repay.'" Merlyn squeezed her eyes shut as she murmured the words. Sometimes truths could be so inconvenient. The rest of Romans 12:19, which she'd memorized on one of her mother's worst nights when she was a child, played through her mind: *Beloved, do not avenge yourselves, but rather give place to wrath; for it is written, "Vengeance is Mine, I will repay," says the Lord.*

"Aren't I supposed to remind you of what's in the Bible?" Celia asked. Merlyn could hear a wry smile in her voice.

Merlyn took a deep breath. "No phone calls."

"You're right. No anti-Reynolds phone calls. Even though he might deserve it, my conscience would protest too. But there will be some pro-Merlyn calls. I will be very careful not to slander Reynolds. I don't want to disappoint God, and I don't want a legal confrontation."

Merlyn's shoulders relaxed. There would be no vengeance. And maybe she'd get the privilege of working with Celia again.

"Several of your clients came to you on my recommendation," Celia reminded her. "They will still want you once they learn you aren't dead. We were there for your design work, not Reynolds's charm. We'll figure things out, so we get what we want—you—and you get what you want—the chance to work with us again. I have a couple of top-notch lawyers on my board of directors. We'll talk again soon." And she was gone.

For a moment, Merlyn sat in the quiet and marveled at the difference one phone call could make.

As she reached for her purse, she caught sight of the floral-covered calendar Winnie had unexpectedly given to her. She pulled it out and hugged it close. How Winnie had known she'd need somewhere to write her appointments, Merlyn couldn't guess. Whether the calendar was symbolic or not—it had been years since she'd kept a paper calendar—it was a wonderful reminder that life never ended until it ended. Up to that last breath, twists and turns abounded.

She couldn't wait to tell Quint the exciting news.

29

Grace

Grace smiled to herself at the expression on Quint's face as he once again watched Merlyn run down the stairs. This budding romance had all the sweetness and excitement that the bride and groom's lacked.

Merlyn practically danced as she greeted Grace. "Isn't it a beautiful day?"

Grace couldn't help but be charmed by the young woman's joy. "It is. Absolutely beautiful." The gloom of the cake disaster was gone, the kitchen was humming with activity, and Rochelle hadn't run in with any more bad news. That was about as good as it got this week.

Merlyn turned to Quint, bouncing on her toes. "You won't believe what happened. Celia Belasco called."

Grace froze at the name of one of her favorite celebrities. She watched Celia Belasco's TV show whenever she could, and she hoped to go to her big conference in October. Celia made the Bible come alive. Even though it was her personal rule not to intrude on her guests' conversations, this time Grace couldn't resist. "You know Celia Belasco?"

Merlyn smiled at Grace, a pretty smile but not nearly as incandescent as the one she'd just given Quint. "I'm her Web designer."

Sue Ann burst into the room, Hailey right behind her, and planted her fist on her hip. "You *were* her Web designer, Merlyn. But now I'm her Web designer. She's mine."

Quint appeared perplexed. "Who's Celia Belasco?"

Grace realized why Quint didn't know who Celia was. While he had been far from home making the world safe for the rest of them, Celia had been growing her ministry, building an army of women who chose to love God, their neighbors, and themselves.

"Just one of the most well-known women in the country," Sue Ann sniffed. "And my client."

"She thought I was dead," Merlyn stated, shaking her head.

Quint frowned. "Why on earth would she think that?"

"Reynolds," Merlyn replied, raising an eyebrow at Sue Ann.

Not unexpectedly, Sue Ann stood her ground as if daring Merlyn to say anything else about Reynolds.

Grace listened in amazement as Merlyn told her tale. Quint appeared shocked, and even Hailey looked a bit surprised.

The only person who didn't seem startled was Sue Ann. Her eyes were hard as she said, "I'm very disappointed in Celia for telling a character assassination story like that."

Grace glanced from Merlyn to Sue Ann and back. She knew which woman she'd put her money on when it came to telling the truth.

Quint grinned at Merlyn. "And you're getting Celia back as a client? Good for you."

Merlyn glowed with excitement. "In two days, I've gone from nothing to a full schedule, thanks to you and Celia." She turned to Grace. "I even have a calendar to write my new appointments in."

Grace smiled. "I knew you'd find a reason for Winnie's gift."

"What gift?" Hailey muttered to Sue Ann. "Did you get a gift?"

"Now you need to come up with a name for your new company," Quint told Merlyn.

"What new company?" Sue Ann's sour voice echoed around the room. "You're not allowed to have a new company. And you're not allowed to contact Celia Belasco or anyone else."

"I didn't contact her," Merlyn said. "She called me."

"As if that makes a difference," Sue Ann huffed. "You can't work with her. She's a client of R&S Design."

"If you say so." Merlyn seemed remarkably assured for someone whose plans were under attack. It sounded as if she knew for a fact that she had Celia in her corner.

"It's the law," Sue Ann insisted, as if trying to convince herself. "You signed the papers. You can't fight the law."

Merlyn shrugged. "We'll see. Are you ready to go, Quint?"

"I am." He gestured toward the front door. "Mom and Dad are waiting. Paige too."

Winnie swept into the room from the direction of the kitchen. "My, but things are buzzing back there. Charlotte and Dean are working together very well, though I'm not sure who's head chef and who's sous-chef."

"It's Charlotte's kitchen," Grace reminded her. "She's in charge."

Winnie nodded. "But I recommend you don't tell Dean."

Grace was smiling when she turned toward the kitchen. The smile fell away when she saw the anger on Sue Ann's face. Hailey stood behind her, eyes narrowed as she watched Quint and Merlyn leave.

Grace sighed. Only two more days and the contentious spirit that filled these two women would be gone.

30

Ashley

Ashley lay facedown on the table and tried not to flinch as the masseuse worked on her back. As the woman corkscrewed a thumb into one very tight knot, Ashley felt her eyes cross at the pain.

"You must be under a lot of stress," the masseuse commented as she ran soothing hands over the spot she'd just skewered. "Your muscles are extremely tight."

No kidding. And her tight muscles were only the tip of the iceberg. Her roiling stomach gurgled impolitely and inconveniently. The lump in her throat made swallowing difficult, forcing her to leave most of the delicious food on her plate untouched. And the hovering cloud of depression made her wonder if she'd ever sport a genuine smile again.

Tears pricked her eyes. The simple truth was Ashley had seen too many princess movies for her own good. Somewhere deep inside, she'd believed the happily-ever-after ending would be hers. It was the automatic reward for good little girls who were kind and nice.

She stifled a bitter laugh. She, Ashley Petersheim, the calm, quiet, nice-to-everyone girl, had become one of the rejected ugly stepsisters instead of Cinderella, and her fairy-tale ending was nothing more than a pipe dream.

The masseuse hit another tender spot, this one in the trapezius.

Ashley scrunched up her face and managed not to groan.

Should she seek out Drake one more time and try to make him understand the mistake he was making? It would be a kindness to him even if it accomplished nothing for her. Or would such a conversation humiliate them both once again? Maybe the smart thing would be to retire from the field with as much grace as she could muster.

The masseuse worked diligently on Ashley's rock-hard trapezius. "Relax," she urged. "Take a deep breath."

Ashley knew relaxing was out of the question, but she could take a deep breath. Her diaphragm and lungs filled. She held the air for a few seconds, then exhaled slowly.

"Again," the masseuse ordered as she set hot stones down the center of Ashley's back.

Ashley did as she was told like the good girl she'd always been.

An hour later, Ashley lay wrapped in seaweed while her mind whirled. *Talk to Drake again. Don't talk to Drake again.*

Maybe she'd fake the flu so she wouldn't have to be in the wedding. She sighed. She'd never faked anything in her life, and she wasn't about to start now. To begin with, she was a lousy liar. When she was with a group playing Two Truths and a Lie, she couldn't even force herself to say the lie.

But the real reason Ashley would march down that aisle in her blue dress was her pride, which wouldn't let her take the easy way out. She might not always win the game, but she always played her best. And she determined to play her best now—if she could only figure out her game plan.

As Ashley smiled through her manicure and pedicure, she felt more confused than ever. By sheer force of will, she smiled through the ride back to the inn. Then she smiled through the rehearsal dinner.

On the ride from dinner back to the inn, Ashley somehow ended up in Drake's car, sitting in the back seat between Colton and PJ. She watched Drake and Paige in the front seat. If she didn't know any better, she'd think they were strangers who had just met, not sweethearts about to marry.

They were ridiculous. She was ridiculous. This whole travesty of a wedding was ridiculous.

And she would no longer be part of it. She was going to tell Drake exactly what she thought. Maybe she'd even tell Paige. She'd say something subtle like, "Don't marry Drake. He's mine."

When they arrived at the inn, Paige jumped from the front seat and latched on to Sue Ann and Hailey before Ashley was even out of the car. No conversation would be possible there.

Colton and PJ got out and headed toward the barn, where the wedding rehearsal would take place.

Ashley slid across the seat. She was about to step from the car when a large hand reached out to her. She glanced up at Drake, so handsome and so kind. And so wrong for Paige.

Even though Ashley didn't need his assistance, she took his hand and let him help her out of the car anyway. He was being polite, and she took advantage of the chance to touch him. Little darts of electricity traveled up her arm when he clasped her hand. Ashley had to speak up once more. This was likely her last chance. "You can't—"

Drake dropped her hand and stepped back. "Don't say it."

His response was like a blow. Ashley put her hand over her heart as if that would protect her from the piercing pain.

Please give me strength, God. Give me courage. And give me the right words.

She clutched at Drake's arm so he couldn't leave before she said her piece, then started again. "You can't marry Paige. You know you can't."

"We've talked about all this before," Drake said, but he didn't pull away from her.

"You don't love her," Ashley said. "You know you don't. I know you don't. She probably knows you don't."

"Omniscient, are you?" he asked, a slight edge to his voice. He obviously didn't like her saying aloud what they both knew.

"About this, yes, I am."

There was a moment of silence. Then Drake yanked his arm from her grasp.

Ashley had to confess her most intimate feelings, even if it made her look like a beggar with her heart in her outstretched hand. She raised her chin and forged ahead. "You can't marry Paige because I'm the one who loves you."

Never had she felt so vulnerable. With her face lit by the light streaming from the barn, Ashley knew Drake could see everything she was feeling. But she couldn't see what he was feeling because his face was in shadow.

"Ashley." Drake reached out and ran the back of his fingers down her cheek.

What did that mean? Did he feel sorry that she felt that way? Did her admission touch his heart? Or did he love her too?

Her cheek tingled from his touch as she waited for him to continue.

When he didn't explain what he meant, she pushed on. "You're thinking you have to go through with the wedding because you somehow gave your word. What would the Repperts think if you backed out? It would be dishonorable, and you're an honorable man. Well, that's wrong. The truth is that marrying Paige would be just plain cruel."

"Cruel?" Drake repeated with a note of surprise.

Ashley nodded. "Paige will be unhappy married to you."

"Thanks," he muttered.

"Don't get all huffy," she replied. "She will. And you'll be unhappy married to her. Who goes into a marriage knowing that?"

"It doesn't have to be that way," Drake said.

"No, it doesn't." Because Ashley offered better. She offered the real thing. She offered love. "There are other options. Don't marry at all." She swallowed the obstruction that appeared in her throat and plunged ahead. It was now or never. "Or you could marry me."

"Ashley," he said, his voice full of distress.

She felt another stab in her heart. He was supposed to say, "What a wonderful idea."

"Okay, you don't love me, so forget that suggestion," Ashley said, trying not to sound crushed. "But you definitely don't love Paige. You can't marry her."

Drake caught her hand and squeezed it. "You're an amazing woman, Ashley Petersheim, strong and outrageously brave." Then he turned and strode toward the barn.

What? That was it? No, it couldn't be. She hadn't changed his mind yet. Panic gripped her. "Where are you going?" she called.

"To be as strong as you. To do the honorable thing."

31

Merlyn

Quint dropped Merlyn by the barn, then took the car to the parking area.

She watched him go and could practically hear her heart purring with contentment. The last thing she'd expected from this trip was what might be the beginning of—well, the beginning of something very special. It made her nervous to even think in terms of a romance blossoming. Her last foray into love had gone so badly. Then again, thank goodness it had gone badly. Otherwise, she wouldn't be getting to know Quint.

Humming happily, she turned to go into the barn.

Someone called her name from around the darkened corner of the building.

Merlyn stopped in the wash of light spilling from the open doors and peered into the gloom. "Who's there?" There was no way she was going to walk into the shadows without knowing who was calling to her.

Reynolds, wearing a peevish expression, peeked around the corner as if he didn't want to be seen. He ducked back out of sight as soon as she recognized him. "I need to talk to you," he hissed.

She took a couple of steps in his direction. "You need to talk to me?" Suddenly, after avoiding her for the past several days, he wanted to talk to her? In the dark? "Well, here I am. Come say whatever you've got to say."

"Not where everyone can see," Reynolds said. "This is a private conversation. Come over here."

"I don't think so," Merlyn said, astonished by his audacity. Why would she talk to him in the light of day, let alone in the shadows? The man was not lacking in gall. Character, yes. Integrity, yes. Nerve, no.

Reynolds didn't respond. Instead, he dashed forward, grabbed her wrist, and pulled her around the corner into the shadows.

"Let me go!" Merlyn tried to yank her arm away, but he tightened his grip. She wasn't frightened. She was furious. "If you don't let go of me this minute, I'll scream."

He laughed. "Don't be ridiculous."

"I promise you I will."

Reynolds must have heard the determination in her voice because he loosened his hold.

Merlyn stepped away from him, rubbing her wrist. "Don't ever touch me again. You lost that privilege the day you turned on me."

"Sorry." He held his hands up, palms out. "I didn't mean to upset you."

As she turned to leave, he lurched toward her again. She glared at him. "You must want me to scream and bring Sue Ann running."

"How would it look to be found in the dark with me?" Reynolds asked. His sneer was visible even in the shadows. "Your less-than-stellar reputation would be dinged yet again."

"And yours wouldn't?" Merlyn shot back. "Of the two of us, you're the one who's engaged."

"Actually, I'll be just fine by the time I finish telling everyone how you came after me and pleaded with me to take you back. When I refused, you tried to frame me to get even."

"You may be the only person who thinks my reputation is less than stellar. Everyone else seems to like me well enough." She stood level with the the corner of the barn, out of the light streaming from the doors but not in the shadows like Reynolds. "Now say what you want to say so I can leave."

He smiled. All vestiges of scorn instantly disappeared, and charm oozed from every pore.

Merlyn was immediately on high alert.

"I think it would be a good idea if you came back to R&M," Reynolds announced.

What? Was he nuts? Merlyn stared at him, dumbfounded. "I thought it was R&S," she finally said.

"It's easy enough to change it back." He smiled again with that easy charm she used to swoon over back when she was a fool.

Duplicitous wasn't a strong enough word for the man. All she could think of was poor Sue Ann defending him against the indefensible. "Why would you want me back after you went to so much trouble getting rid of me?"

"We were a strong team, you and me," Reynolds said, ignoring her question. "You blossomed under my leadership."

"There might be a certain truth there," Merlyn agreed. Though she'd come to realize he'd benefitted more from her skills than she had from his.

"I think it's to your advantage to work with me again," he continued.

"To my advantage?" she asked. "How?"

Reynolds seemed a bit uncomfortable. "I would again be in the position to guide you. You know I've always appreciated your potential and your talent."

"No, I don't know that," Merlyn said, crossing her arms over her chest.

He snorted. "You aren't stupid. You know you're good."

"I do, but I didn't think you knew."

"Well, I do." His tone was waspish. He cleared his throat and resumed his pleasant and honeyed tone. "I would like you to come back to work."

Of course he would. He needed to rehire her before the Celia avalanche started. "Did it hurt to say that?"

Movement off to the side caught her eye. Quint had come from the parking area. He stopped a few feet from her and quirked an eyebrow in question.

She held up a finger, holding it around the corner of the barn so Reynolds couldn't see.

Quint nodded, then leaned against the side of the barn and crossed one foot over the other at the ankles. He was more handsome than any hero on a romance book cover.

Reynolds, unaware he had an eavesdropper, went on. "I made a mistake, Merlyn. There. I said it. Is that what you wanted?"

She looked Reynolds in the eye. "It is sweet to hear. Thank you."

Reynolds thought he'd won with his confession and her acknowledgment of it. She could see it in his smile, his relaxed manner, and his charm, which he cranked up to full blast. "So you're coming back." He made it a statement. He really thought he had her.

"What about Sue Ann?" she asked.

"What about her?"

"You're going to do to her what you did to me?"

The charm dimmed. He obviously didn't like being challenged. "How I deal with Sue Ann is my own business."

"You know she genuinely loves you," Merlyn persisted.

"She was a mistake," Reynolds said. "You were the woman of my heart."

"Were?"

Anger flashed over his face. "You *are* the woman of my heart," he corrected.

She glanced over at Quint. He winked at her, and she couldn't help but smile.

Reynolds, as full of himself as always, assumed the smile was for him and his declaration. He reached for her hand.

Merlyn stuffed her hand into her pocket. "Why should I trust you?" She gave Reynolds her steeliest gaze. "Everything we had together was a lie. Why should I believe it's real this time around? Do you think I'm that stupid?"

Reynolds managed to appear crushed, though the rigidity of his shoulders and his balled fists shouted rage. "Come on, sweetheart," he coaxed. "You know you can trust me."

She gaped at him, astounded at his nerve. "No, I don't. You used me. Then you threw me away. How can you expect me to act like that didn't happen?"

"I said I was sorry for my misjudgment."

As if an insincere apology made it all better. Merlyn studied him, a handsome man with nothing but scheming and vanity inside. Then she glanced over at Quint, currently crouching to scratch a delighted Winston with Locky impatiently waiting his turn. What a contrast.

"You may have a less-than-stellar background—" Reynolds said.

"Are we really back to that again?" Merlyn asked.

"But you are rising above it," Reynolds went on as if she hadn't interrupted him. "You have talent, and I appreciate that. You have a forgiving heart, and I love that."

"Are you saying you're willing to put up with Trailer Girl for the websites I can design for you?" Merlyn asked. "So you can make money off my talent, even if I come from such humble beginnings?"

"Yes, because you're no longer Trailer Girl," Reynolds answered.

"I'll always be Trailer Girl. Don't you know that? She's part of who I am." She glanced at Quint, who was standing against the barn again—so solid, so dependable, so handsome.

Quint smiled at her. He accepted that part of her that would always be Trailer Girl.

"What are you looking at? Is someone over there?" Reynolds rounded the corner of the barn and saw Quint.

As Quint shifted his gaze from Merlyn to Reynolds, his pleasant expression changed to contempt.

Reynolds took a step back, and his features hardened. He turned to Merlyn and hissed, "You think someone like him is going to show any real interest in someone like you? Get over yourself. He's using you for entertainment while we're here. You think he's going to talk to you when we get back to Reynolds? If so, you're even more foolish than I thought."

Quint was at Merlyn's side before Reynolds finished speaking. He eyed Reynolds with disdain as he put a protective arm around her shoulders. "I would be delighted if someone like Merlyn shows an interest in me." He smiled at her. "They don't come any better."

Without another word to Reynolds, they strolled into the barn together.

32

Paige

Paige stood with Sue Ann and Hailey on what would be the dance floor at the reception and scanned the barn for her father. They still needed to practice for their special dance, but she didn't want to do it when anyone else was around. Maybe they could do it early tomorrow morning.

Tomorrow. Her wedding day. Her heart seized. Black dots danced before her eyes, and she gripped the back of a nearby chair.

"You're going to be such a beautiful bride," Sue Ann said sincerely.

"Thank you." Paige forced herself to smile. Too bad she didn't feel beautiful. Aside from the panic of nearly fainting, she felt flat. False. Foolish. She'd worked herself into a corner she didn't know how to get out of, but at least the black spots dancing before her eyes were receding.

"You'll be a beautiful bride yourself," Paige told Sue Ann, meaning it. Too bad the groom would be Reynolds.

As if on cue, Reynolds approached the group. Paige thought he appeared pale and put out.

"I've started the hunt for my bridal gown," Sue Ann admitted with a simpering smile at Reynolds.

Paige sighed and managed a sliver of sorrow for her friend. Sue Ann was still excited to marry a man who played loose with both business ethics and people's feelings. How did she know he wouldn't turn on her someday?

At least Drake would never stab her in the back. Paige studied the floor. But she was stabbing him, using him, taking advantage of his streak of honor. She finally felt something. Self-loathing.

Hailey held the bouquet of ribbons taken from Paige's bridal shower gifts. She twirled it in her hands. "When I marry Quint, I . . ."

Paige let Hailey's words fade. When she married Quint? Who was she kidding? Quint was standing by the barn door, his attention focused on something Merlyn was saying. They were holding hands as they talked. Hailey didn't have a chance, had probably never had a chance.

Paige had considered Sue Ann and Hailey her best friends since kindergarten. They used to call themselves The Triumphs back in high school because they triumphed in whatever they did. They came from money. They had prominent families, nice families who fawned over them. They had gotten pretty much everything they wanted—clothes, cars, electronics, educations, trips. And this was what their lives had come to?

Sue Ann was marrying an untrustworthy man who was all charm and no substance. The saddest thing was that she thought she was the luckiest woman alive to have him.

Hailey was still chasing Quint after more than ten years of his lack of interest. She seemed to think that because she wanted him, he would return the favor. After all, she always got everything she wanted. If she wanted Quint, she'd get him. Trouble was, he wasn't a mindless acquisition to be purchased with enough money.

And there was her own mess of a life. Paige wasn't as gossipy and critical as Sue Ann and Hailey, but she was strong-willed and selfish. She was nowhere near as nice as Ashley or as worthy as Merlyn. She was too intent on molding people to her plans, and she knew how to work her family to get what she wanted. This disaster of a wedding was a case in point.

"I love Drake," she'd told her parents. "I can't stand being apart from him. We want to marry in two months."

Drake had stood beside her in the family room, never contradicting her but never encouraging her either.

Despite his lack of verbal support, they managed to convince her parents, who were already accustomed to giving her whatever she wanted. Mom jumped in with both feet, doing everything she could to make the rushed wedding an event to remember.

Dad spent a small fortune to provide the very best for her—from the inn to her dress to the flowers and all the other trappings of a wedding made more important than the marriage. He was even treating them to a week in the Caribbean as a wedding present. It frustrated her that Drake had merely thanked her father and accepted the trip as if they deserved it.

They did not. At least she did not.

Paige glanced around for Drake, but she didn't see him. It didn't matter. He'd show up when it was time to begin. He always did what he was supposed to do, sort of like her. Well, usually.

She'd acted uncharacteristically spontaneous once, and it hadn't worked out well. But she'd felt alive then. Excited. She'd anticipated each morning, enjoyed each day, savored every night—until she hadn't.

So here Paige was, about to marry a man she didn't love, but she'd be safe. As much as she told herself that safe was good, she missed that inner vibrancy. Drake would never be able to give her that feeling of liveliness. She blinked, trying desperately to keep her tears at bay.

"Oh, look." Hailey nudged Sue Ann with her elbow. "She's so happy she's crying. Isn't that sweet?"

Paige swallowed a sharp retort. She wished Hailey would get a grip.

Drake stalked into the barn.

Paige did a double take. Drake never stalked. He always moved steadily and smoothly. He lived his life in moderation, and his emotions were without peaks or valleys. Drake was pleasant, easy to be around, and accommodating. His agreeable personality was one of the reasons she'd decided to marry him.

She respected Drake. He, like Merlyn, came from a difficult background, and like her he'd risen above it by his own will and hard work. Paige respected him in the same way she respected Merlyn. And wasn't that a romantic thought?

Movement at the door drew her attention. Ashley trudged into the barn, her face pale. Something about her posture screamed defeat. How unusual. Ashley was such a positive person. Sometimes Hailey mocked her for being so nice, but Paige had always liked her for that very reason. Too many people were selfish and self-serving, so people like Ashley were treasures.

Ashley followed Drake with her eyes, and *yearning* was the only word that described her expression. As Paige glanced from one to the other, she felt her jaw drop.

Ashley had a thing for Drake? Since when? Paige knew Drake had been dating someone before their engagement, but she hadn't given it a thought when she decided to marry him. Was sweet Ashley the woman she'd undercut? She suddenly felt sick to her stomach.

"Excuse me for a minute," Paige said to Sue Ann and Hailey and fled to the ladies' room. She locked herself in a stall and dropped her face into her hands. What had she done?

God, help me! She didn't even know what to ask Him for. Rescue? Courage? An alien invasion? A life-threatening disease that struck by tomorrow morning?

She heard the ladies' room door open and knew she could no longer hide.

"Paige, are you okay?" Sue Ann asked.

"I'll be right out," Paige called.

"I was afraid you were sick." Sue Ann sounded concerned. "Like maybe you ate something at dinner that upset your stomach."

Paige walked from the stall with her patented phony smile in place. "Thanks for checking on me. I'm fine."

"What a relief," Sue Ann said.

Paige washed her hands and watched the high-powered dryer push the skin on the back of her hands around. How sad was it that the big entertainment of her wedding rehearsal night was the rippling of her skin?

"Let's get back out there," Sue Ann said. "Everyone's waiting for you."

As Paige followed her to the dance floor, she searched for Drake. He was in a serious conversation with her mother and father. She needed to talk to them too, so she headed in their direction.

A man with broad shoulders and long dark hair burst through the door, a look of determination on his rugged face. His appearance was so sudden it startled her.

Paige blinked and blinked again. Surely she was hallucinating. But he didn't disappear. Her heart began to race, and she covered her mouth with both hands. She stood there, unable to move, unable to think, unable to breathe as she drank in the man before her.

A bandage sat at a rakish angle at his hairline. He used a cane, and it appeared small and bothersome in his hand. Her stomach flipped when she realized he'd been hurt and she hadn't even known. She should have been sitting by his hospital bed, holding his hand, cheering him up, worrying about his recovery.

Tears blurred her vision. She'd been faithless, and she didn't deserve him.

But he was here anyway.

"Strobinski," Quint said as he moved toward the man, pulling Merlyn with him. "I was so worried about you and relieved when I heard you'd been rescued." Her brother caught him in a big hug complete with a few pats on the back. "I'm glad to see you, but should you be up and about?"

"I'm not here for you." Bryce Strobinski scanned the room. He spotted Paige and strode toward her. "I'm here for my wife."

33

Ashley

Ashley followed Drake into the barn, pulled a chair from the first table she reached, and collapsed into it.

The Repperts and Rochelle stood nearby talking to the officiant. Drake went directly to the Repperts and was welcomed with smiles and hugs. They were the family he wanted, and she couldn't blame him. They were wonderful people who would make him their son. No more being on the fringes. No more wondering where he belonged.

Ashley couldn't stand to watch, so she faced the other way in the chair and glanced around without real interest. Under other circumstances, she'd be charmed by the juxtaposition of the rough-hewn barn and the elegant crystal chandeliers and swags of material draped over the rafters. Round tables with white cloths filled both sides of the barn with an open area down the center. At one end stood an arbor festooned with clouds of white tulle. Rows of white chairs faced the arbor, awaiting tomorrow's guests. It would be even lovelier when the florist added the flowers in the morning.

As she stared morosely at the chandeliers shooting rainbows about the room, Drake appeared at her side.

Ashley wondered why he was approaching her. Hadn't he hurt her enough? "What do you want?" she asked. She hoped she sounded angry, but she felt too broken to muster anything as strong as anger.

He didn't say anything as he sank into the chair next to hers, leaned forward, and rested his arms on his knees.

She studied him. The air around him seemed to crackle and shimmer. Despite her anger, she grew concerned. "Are you all right?"

Drake grinned. "Never better."

Ashley tried to resent his smile, but it took too much energy. "Go smile somewhere else."

He made no move to leave. Instead, he continued grinning at her.

She glared at him. "Now." Before she burst into tears and thoroughly humiliated herself.

"I need to talk to Paige," Drake said.

"Of course you do. So why are you telling me?" Ashley snapped. "Go talk to her."

Instead of backing off at her snippy tone, Drake leaned even closer. Their knees touched. It was only a little thing, but it was deliberate and inappropriate for a man about to marry another.

"And then I need to speak with you," he said, his voice soft and intimate.

Her head jerked up. She couldn't believe how inappropriate he was acting.

"Will you please wait here for me?" Drake asked.

It was an ordinary question, but it caused a flutter of hope in her heart, especially when he smiled at her like he used to back when he came to Charlotte to see her. Back when he said he enjoyed her, whatever that meant.

"Why should I wait for you?" Ashley demanded. She believed if she sounded hostile enough, he'd go away, and the hope would die before it burned her once again.

"No reason. But I hope you will." For the briefest moment, Drake closed his hand over hers and squeezed. When he released her, he kept his hand below the table and flashed her the sign for "I love you."

Ashley sat there, dumbfounded.

When their eyes connected, he winked at her.

Now the hope in her heart wasn't just fluttering. It soared. "I'll be right here," Ashley whispered.

As Drake rose, a dark-haired man with a cane burst into the barn. Quint apparently knew him, but Ashley couldn't help thinking that crashing a wedding rehearsal was not something that would be approved by Miss Manners.

Then the dark-haired man called Paige his wife.

34

Paige

Paige knew everyone in the barn was gaping at her, but all she saw was Bryce. She had been so sure she'd never set eyes on him again. The more time passed, the more she was convinced he'd used her the way Reynolds had used Merlyn. Not the business part. The broken heart part.

As Bryce marched toward Paige, he limped with every step, pain tightening his mouth. She was startled to notice that he was thinner than the last time she'd seen him. He had dark circles under his eyes, and he was much too pale.

Finally unfrozen, Paige took a step toward Bryce. "You should be in a wheelchair."

He snorted.

"Or on crutches."

"More trouble than they're worth."

Paige shook her head, but secretly she was glad he was still the feisty, cocky man she'd fallen in love with. The polar opposite of Drake.

He stopped in front of her and gazed at her with his crooked smile, his eyes warm. "My beautiful wife. There were so many times when I was afraid I'd never see you again."

His voice made her melt inside. "I'm not your wife. We're not married." Paige's voice was rough with emotion. She had to swallow before she could continue. "It was all a joke. You said so yourself."

Their last conversation was a sound loop she'd played over and over in her mind.

"What do you mean you won't come to California with me?" Bryce had asked her, bewildered.

"You have to come to South Carolina with me," Paige argued. "I want to have a real wedding." What woman didn't?

"You think we didn't have a real wedding?"

"Married by an Elvis impersonator?" Paige said. "That's not real."

"It was real to me," he said.

"I want the gown, the excitement. I want it all."

"I thought we had it all."

"Well, yeah. But—"

"But this marriage is a joke?" Bryce interrupted. "Is that what you're saying?"

That was when her fear began. Paige had known him for only two days before she married him. What if he wasn't what she thought?

It had all started while Paige was on vacation in California. She had dinner with Quint and several of his friends and fellow SEALs. Quint and the others had left, but Bryce had stayed. Paige extended her vacation for a quick trip to Las Vegas with him. And that was where they got married.

"No, it's not a joke," Paige said. "We're not a joke. Are we?"

"Oh, it's a great big joke all right." And Bryce stormed out of the room.

Paige sat on the bed and waited for him to come back. Panic set in after an hour, and she went to search for him. She didn't need a big wedding. She just needed him. This marriage wasn't a joke. It was real. Wasn't it? But she'd never found Bryce, and he'd never contacted her again.

She'd been devastated. Her beautiful honeymoon was no more

than a cheap, sleazy few days with a guy who'd tricked her? And she'd been foolish enough to fall right into his arms. She was the joke.

So Paige had come home and planned her great big wedding. She'd show him.

Now here she was, the night before that wedding, face-to-face with the man who'd shattered her heart.

Bryce reached out and brushed her hair behind her ear. "Paige, our marriage was real. It is real."

She closed her eyes at his touch, a touch she had never expected to feel again. "Is it? You left me. One fight and you walked out."

"That was my stupid pride. I'll never do it again, I promise. I learned my lesson." His voice was soft, and he cupped her face in his hand. "I've missed you so much."

"I went looking for you, but I couldn't find you," Paige said. She wanted him to understand her fear, her distress. "When I came back to the room, you were gone. Duffel bag, clothes, everything."

"I had to go. I didn't have a choice. It was wheels up." Bryce cocked his head. "Didn't Quint tell you? He was there when we took off."

She couldn't believe it. Quint knew and said nothing?

Bryce glanced over his shoulder at Quint. "What happened?"

Quint frowned. "You mean when you yelled, 'Tell her I'll be back as soon as I can,' you were talking about my sister?"

Bryce nodded. "Who else?"

"How was I supposed to know that?" Quint asked. "I remember being impressed that you finally had a woman in your life, but I had no idea that woman was Paige. You left out that little detail." He transferred his gaze to his sister. "So did you."

Paige hung her head. She hadn't told anyone in her family about her marriage. At the time, she liked holding the secret close to her heart. They'd learn about it soon enough, but for that small slice of time, it was just her and Bryce, Mr. and Mrs. Strobinski. After Bryce disappeared, she was glad she hadn't told them. It saved her the humiliation of confessing she'd been jilted.

Bryce turned to Paige, his mouth quirking up on one side in that way she loved. "You're a wonderful woman, even though you were trying to commit bigamy."

"I'm sorry," she whispered. "But you—" Her voice broke. She grabbed his hand and held on. "You've been gone for over two months without a word."

"I was in the hospital," he said, holding out his cane.

"For two months?" Paige asked, surprised.

"My team got me out of a rebel prison four days ago," Bryce replied. "I've only been back in the States for three days, two of them in the hospital."

She gently touched the bandage and indicated his foot. "Are you all right?"

"I'll be about 95 percent," he answered, sounding resigned to his fate.

Paige knew that was better than 99.5 percent of regular men, but it wasn't enough for the SEALs. "The Navy's letting you go," she said quietly.

Bryce nodded. "You're married to a civilian. At least you will be when the paperwork goes through."

"I'm so sorry." She knew it had to be a knife in his heart.

"We'll figure it out," he said. "We have lots of time to talk about options."

Paige was certain the last thing he wanted was sympathy, so she said, "If you've been home for three days, how come you didn't call me?"

"I tried, but your phone kept sending me straight to voice mail, which was full." Bryce narrowed his eyes. "Probably all those best wishes for your upcoming wedding."

She colored. That was probably right.

"Then I called your brother, and he told me the family was here for your destination wedding." His expression was half disbelief and half hurt. "Imagine my surprise when I learned that my wife was getting married to someone else."

Paige stared at the floor because she couldn't meet his eyes. "I wanted to show you."

Bryce lifted her chin so she couldn't avoid his gaze. "You wanted to show me what?"

"That someone would marry me for real."

He kissed her. "Someone already did marry you for real." He smoothed a hand over her hair. "It was thoughts of you that kept me sane in that rebel jail. It was the thought of coming home to you that gave me courage through the torture. I'd picture you, my wife, and I didn't break."

With a sob, Paige threw herself into his arms. "I'm sorry."

He held her close and whispered in her ear, "I love you with all my heart."

Merlyn

Quint took a step toward Bryce Strobinski.

Merlyn caught Quint's arm. She had no idea what was on his mind or what he intended to say, but it was clear that Paige and Bryce needed time alone. "Not now. Come and sit with me." She sat down at the nearest table.

With a sigh, Quint sank into the chair beside Merlyn.

She patted his hand. "It'll be fine. She'll be fine. Look at her."

Paige glowed, her face full of the joy and happiness that had been missing. She and Bryce walked slowly toward the barn door. He gripped his cane with one hand, and with the other, he held Paige's hand as if he'd never let go.

"Poor Mom and Dad. I'd better go see if I can do anything for them." Quint stood and went over to them.

Merlyn followed and joined them. James seemed confused. His reaction wasn't surprising since he'd thought everything was fine with the elaborate wedding he was paying for. Sonja regarded Bryce with a dubious expression.

"Are you two okay?" Quint asked his parents.

Before they could answer, Bryce and Paige approached.

Bryce held out his hand. "Mr. Reppert, it's a privilege to meet you, sir."

James ignored Bryce's outstretched hand and gave him a hard stare, then glanced at his smiling daughter.

"I love him, and I hope you'll love him too," Paige told her dad. "But whatever you say, I'm keeping him forever and ever."

"And I love her, sir," Bryce said. "Make no mistake about that. I'll take good care of her."

James still seemed skeptical, but he shook Bryce's hand.

Paige threw her arms around her father's neck and gave him a kiss on the cheek. "Thank you. It'll be great. You'll see."

"Mrs. Reppert," Bryce said, holding out his hand, "it's a pleasure to meet you too."

Sonja disregarded his gesture and turned to Paige. "So he's been in your head and heart this whole time?"

Paige grabbed Bryce's arm and held on tight. She nodded.

Sonja nodded back. She frowned at Bryce. "If you hurt her again, I'll hunt you down."

"*We'll* hunt you down," James corrected.

Bryce met their gazes. "I understand. I'll never again give you a reason to."

"Good," Sonja said very seriously. She broke into a smile. "Now give me a hug, both of you, and get out of here." She warmly embraced Paige, then Bryce.

Bryce caught Paige's hand, and the beaming couple strode from the barn.

It struck Merlyn that Paige finally appeared as happy as she should have been all along.

When they disappeared into the darkness, Merlyn and Quint talked to his parents for a few minutes and then sat down across from Ashley and Drake at the table.

"Strobe and Paige," Quint mumbled, apparently still in shock.

Merlyn felt sudden concern. "You do like him, don't you? He is a good man?"

"The best."

Colton pulled up a chair beside Quint. "Is he good enough for her?"

"Yeah, he's a great guy," Quint replied. "We were on the same team for five years. I trust him with my life."

"Good," Colton said, then turned to Drake. "Are you okay?"

Merlyn breathed a sigh of relief. She'd been wondering who would address the elephant in the room.

"I'm fine," Drake said. "A little bit stunned but fine." He seemed remarkably unfazed after watching another man walk off with his bride.

"Really?" Colton pressed, sounding unconvinced.

Ashley poked Drake in the side. "Now you don't have to have that talk with Paige."

Drake tipped his head in acknowledgment. "I wasted all that energy worrying that I'd hurt her."

Colton frowned. "What talk with Paige? How would you hurt her?"

Drake twisted in his seat, and his shoulder pressed against Ashley's.

For the first time Merlyn noticed Drake and Ashley were clasping hands beneath the table. Merlyn studied Ashley's luminous and lovely face. She then considered Drake and decided he appeared relaxed and happy rather than determined and noble.

So Ashley loved Drake. No wonder she'd been crying when she thought he was going to marry Paige. But apparently Drake loved Ashley back. Someday maybe Ashley would tell her the story of how he'd finally realized it.

Merlyn glanced around the room. Were there any other surprises lurking?

Hailey, Sue Ann, Reynolds, and PJ pulled up chairs at the table. At the same time, James and Sonja, with Rochelle and the officiant at their side, stopped to say goodbye.

Quint and Colton rose and kissed their mother.

Sonja surprised Merlyn by bending and bussing her cheek. Merlyn smiled. She felt blessed to be the recipient of this kind woman's affection and approval.

When they left, Colton turned to Drake and repeated, "What talk with Paige?"

Drake smiled at Ashley. "I was going to tell Paige I couldn't marry her."

Colton crossed his arms and glared at him. "Why not?"

"It doesn't matter anymore," Quint told his brother.

Drake answered anyway. "I'm in love with someone else."

Ashley's smile mirrored Drake's as she leaned into him.

Colton seemed disconcerted.

Quint reached out and patted his brother's shoulder as he might to calm Winston or Locky. "It's a moot point, anyway. Paige doesn't want to marry Drake either. Apparently, she's already married."

"That's true," Colton said. "My head is spinning."

"Well, at least I don't have to worry about the ruffled dress." Merlyn felt as if a weight had been lifted off her shoulders. "And the little birdcage hat."

Merlyn heard a hiss from the other side of the table, though she couldn't tell who it came from. "It's a shame though, isn't it?" she asked Ashley. "You saw how unique it was." She turned her head so only Ashley could see her wink.

"It was a thing of rare beauty," Ashley agreed.

Merlyn nodded. "Such a generous gift."

"She got another gift?" Hailey muttered to Sue Ann.

"Someone gave you a dress to wear in the wedding?" Sue Ann asked, her eyes flashing. "That's quite the gift."

"And a cute little birdcage hat," Merlyn added. She removed Sue Ann from her list of suspects. She seemed too upset at what she viewed as preferential treatment.

"But we're supposed to wear flowers in our hair," Hailey pointed out.

"I know." Merlyn tried to sound perplexed even as she mentally drew a line through Hailey's name. "Can you tell me who would know my dress size, know about the robin's-egg blue, but not know about the flowers? Oh, and who would want me to be embarrassed by wearing something truly ugly and would write *Marilyn* on the box to make me think it came from Sonja? Who could the unkind culprit possibly be?"

With these clues, everyone at the table turned to Reynolds.

He leaned back and held up his hands. "It was only a joke."

"You bought her a dress?" Sue Ann's voice was a combination of jealousy and disbelief. "Why in the world would you do that?"

"Don't let it upset you." Reynolds reached a hand toward her. "Like I said, it was just a joke."

Sue Ann batted his hand away. "Not a very good one," she said tartly.

"Come on," Reynolds cajoled, his tone holding a distinct edge. He didn't seem to be taking Sue Ann's anger well, but then as Merlyn knew, he never took any criticism well. "Let it go. It was only a little jab at her for trying to take our clients."

Merlyn considered reminding him that the dress came well before the client invitations, but she decided it wasn't worth mentioning. He was and probably always would be selfish and self-serving. That was all there was to it.

Then Merlyn remembered something about the incident. "How did you get into my room?" she asked Reynolds. "The door was locked."

Sue Ann gasped. "You were in her room?"

"I might have borrowed a key from the desk," Reynolds said quickly, then continued to plead his case with Sue Ann. "You know you're the one for me. That dress isn't worth all this drama she's making of it."

Merlyn felt her anger surge. He was going to make believe his poor joke was all her fault? And Sue Ann was going to buy his line?

"And she's definitely not worth your time and attention." Reynolds flicked a disdainful look in Merlyn's direction.

Quint stood and leaned across the table toward Reynolds. "If she's not worth your time and attention, then why were you begging her to come back to R&M less than an hour ago?"

Reynolds fell back in his chair, eyes wide with surprise and maybe a touch of fear.

"What?" Sue Ann stared at her fiancé, her face a study in hurt and confusion. "But we're R&S, not R&M. Reynolds and Sue Ann. You and me."

"You don't understand," Reynolds said. His face turned white while his ears turned red. "It's not what it sounds like."

"Then please clarify." Sue Ann crossed her arms over her chest. "Did you or did you not ask her back?"

Reynolds didn't respond. He couldn't hide the truth of his guilt in his expression.

Sue Ann wilted. She had definitely caught a glimpse of the unethical schemer she was engaged to. "How could you do that?" A world of hurt rang in her voice.

Merlyn knew exactly how Sue Ann felt, but she didn't say anything because she was certain she was the last person Sue Ann wanted sympathy from.

Hailey glared at Reynolds. She might hate Merlyn for her own obscure reasons, but she loved Sue Ann as a sister. She got up, aiming her considerable store of malice at Reynolds. "You despicable sleazebag! You were going to throw Sue Ann under the bus for *her*?" She swept a hand contemptuously toward Merlyn.

Merlyn rolled her eyes. Even in the chaos of tonight, some things remained constant.

Sue Ann burst into tears.

Hailey bent over Sue Ann, full of concern and compassion. "Let's get out of here." She put an arm around her friend and helped her from her chair.

As they walked from the barn, Sue Ann muttered through her tears, "My father warned me about him. I should have listened."

In the silence that followed, everyone turned to Reynolds.

He tried to stare them all down for about five seconds before he seemed to realize the futility of that move. He rose with a grumble and left.

Quint sat back and grinned. "And I was afraid coming home would be boring."

36

Grace

Grace stood in the back of the barn Saturday afternoon and watched the beautiful wedding. Everything seemed to go as planned except there was a new groom. He was a rugged-looking man dressed in Navy whites, and wherever he'd come from, he was definitely the bride's true love. Paige was radiant.

The original groom sat in the first row and kept smiling at Ashley, who stood as one of the two female attendants.

Bright and early this morning, Sue Ann and Hailey had stormed out of the inn. Grace had to admit she was relieved to see them go, even though she had no idea what had brought on their sudden departure. Apparently, she'd missed a lot of drama last night by going to the potluck supper at church instead of the rehearsal in the barn.

Merlyn was now the maid of honor. She was lovely in an understated dress of robin's-egg blue that was perfect for her classic beauty. A halo of daisies and rosebuds sat on her froth of curls, its ribbons flowing down her back, and she held a bouquet of matching daisies and rosebuds. The bride's bouquet was made up of the same flowers with scarlet alstroemeria added.

Grace had to grin at the way the best man in a morning suit that finally fit kept staring at Merlyn.

Reynolds was also missing from the group, but no one seemed to even notice, let alone mind.

"They're already married," Rochelle whispered to Grace. "Can you believe it? I almost helped her commit bigamy."

"I don't think anyone would have held you responsible," Grace said. "Besides, it all seems to have worked out quite well. You did a great job. Everything's lovely."

"When I left last night, I was afraid there wouldn't be a wedding. I came this morning all set to recommend a recommitment service—might as well salvage as much as we could—and I found they'd already decided to do just that." Rochelle sighed happily. "I love a good love story, and this is one of the best." On that note, she bustled off to do the next thing on her checklist.

"It sure is a good love story," Winnie said. "And what a beautiful event."

"The best is yet to come," Charlotte murmured as she came up behind them dressed in her white chef's jacket. "Wait until you see the feast Dean and I pulled off."

"Maybe we should sample the food to make sure everything is up to snuff," Grace suggested.

"Ha!" Charlotte gently bumped Grace. "As if we'd ever offer anything but the highest quality."

Winnie laughed and slid an arm around both sisters. "I love you girls."

Grace smiled. "We love you too."

And she loved her life. She was thankful for her aunt and sister and for all their intriguing guests. There were always wonderful surprises in store at the Magnolia Harbor Inn.

Victorian Mansion Flower Shop Mysteries™

Set on sparkling Puget Sound in the cozy island town of Turtle Cove, Washington, the stories in this enthralling series are good old-fashioned whodunits chock-full of fascinating family secrets, breathtaking scenery, heartwarming discoveries, and the unbreakable bonds of female friendships.

If you love the great outdoors, gardens, birds, flowers, and a good mystery book . . . then you'll love Annie's *Victorian Mansion Flower Shop Mysteries!*

AnniesFiction.com